Abigail looked down at the ring winking back at her from her finger. When the right man comes along, grab him, she reflected. It was good advice, and she had got the right man. She smiled happily. Yes, Rupert was the perfect man, there was nothing to worry about.

Still smiling, she stepped into the corridor, only to bump into Greg as he made his way back to the ward. Yes, she thought again, Rupert is the right man, not like you, Mr Lincoln, who'll be going back to America at the end of the year, no doubt leaving a trail of broken hearts behind you!

He had one of his black moody expressions on his face, but undeterred, Abigail smiled sweetly. 'Goodnight, Mr Lincoln,' she said gaily, resisting the sudden impulse to wave her diamonds defiantly under his nose.

'Why the Mr Lincoln bit?' he asked, still looking bad-tempered.

'I'm feeling formal,' said Abigail, adding cheekily, 'I *am* English, you know!'

'*Don't* I know!' replied Greg sarcastically.

It was Abigail's turn to glower at his retreating back. He'd had the last word as usual!

Ann Jennings has been married for thirty two years and worked in a hospital for fourteen years—accounting for the technicalities accurately described in her hospital romances. Her son is a doctor and often provides her with amusing titbits of information. Hospitals are romantic places she maintains, romance blossoms where two people share a common interest. *Sold to the Surgeon* is her eighth Doctor Nurse Romance. Recent titles include *Doctor's Orders, Nurse on Loan* and *Really, Doctor!*.

SOLD TO THE SURGEON

BY

ANN   JENNINGS

MILLS & BOON LIMITED
ETON HOUSE   18-24 PARADISE ROAD
RICHMOND   SURREY   TW9 1SR

First published in Great Britain 1988
by Mills & Boon Limited

© Ann Jennings 1988

Australian copyright 1988
Philippine copyright 1988
This edition 1988

ISBN 0 263 76174 6

Set in Times 10 on 11½ pt.
03 – 8809 – 58943

Typeset in Great Britain by JCL Graphics, Bristol

Made and printed in Great Britain

CHAPTER ONE

'IF THAT GIRL drops anything else I shall scream!' Sister Collins' small birdlike frame shook with suppressed anger. 'For goodness' sake, Staff, go and sort her out. Let's try to get some semblance of order on this ward, even if we have only just moved in.'

Abigail Pointer nodded her blonde head; she felt sorry for Sister Collins, even if she was rather a dragon. It was midsummer and very hot, and Abigail felt exhausted herself, so she knew how Sister Collins, who was near to retirement, must be feeling.

'Yes, Sister—don't worry. Between us we'll get it cleared up.'

'Between you!' Sister Collins snorted derisively. 'I'd rather you did it, Staff. Just let Student Nurse Parkins watch you, that way she can't do any more damage!'

As her trim figure sped down the corridor towards the ward kitchen where the noise had originated from, Abigail couldn't help smiling to herself. Poor Student Nurse Parkins, she had an uncanny aptitude for making a mess of everything, and today of all days was definitely not one of Sister's best days! They had just moved into the new ENT ward, in a brand new wing of the County General Hospital, just across the road from the old block, which now stood silent and empty. Although the number of patients had been kept to the absolute minimum for the transfer, it had still been difficult, and Sister Collins could never bear to have her

5

routine upset at the best of times.

Abigail smiled again. Today the routine had been well and truly upset, and she doubted if anything would ever be the same again. For a start, they had changed from the old-fashioned long straight 'Nightingale' type of ward to the new type of wards, consisting of six and four-bedded rooms, plus a few single rooms for the very sick patients, most of which were opposite the nursing station. The worst thing of all, as far as Sister Collins was concerned, was that the office at the far end of the corridor, the one she'd had her eye on, had been arbitrarily commandeered by the new American consultant, Mr Greg Lincoln, who had just arrived at the County General on an exchange.

They had swopped their pleasant, if rather insipid, young consultant, Mr Wilberforce, for this dynamic young American. A little bit too dynamic for Sister Collins, Abigail surmised shrewdly.

She had always got her way with all the consultants before; the older ones had fallen in with her wishes for as long as anyone could remember. They never even did formal ward rounds, just informal visits to their patients, because Sister Collins couldn't stand having her ward upset by the rigours of a ward round! When Mr Wilberforce had been appointed, he hadn't stood a chance. Sister Collins had determinedly ridden roughshod over him, and he had dutifully toed the line. Now, apparently, it was she who was being overridden, and although Abigail had yet to meet the new consultant, she had heard all this from Sue Parkins, their disastrous student nurse.

Her slim form turned the corner swiftly, and went into the ward kitchen. Simultaneously she heard Sue's voice saying, 'Nothing is broken, Staff, but I've just spilt a lot of. . .oooh!'

There was also a male voice with a distinct American twang to it saying, 'Be careful, there's a. . .'

Too late—the rubber on the soles of her shoes went skidding immediately she stepped into the kitchen, straight into a huge puddle of milk. Feeling herself losing her balance, Abigail grabbed at the first thing that came to hand — a white coat. Vaguely she was aware of someone cursing as she hung on trying to save herself, but it was impossible. Down she went, dragging the unfortunate occupant of the white coat with her.

The sticky wetness of the milk soaked through her pale uniform as she slithered on her back across the ward kitchen floor, and a blurred impression of pungent after shave assailed her nostrils, as a heavy form slid with her— cursing all the way!

'Is everyone in this darned hospital mad?' demanded a deep and very angry voice.

Abigail found herself staring into a pair of dark brown, annoyed eyes.

'Oh, you must be Mr Lincoln,' she said. It was an idiotic thing to say, she knew that as soon as she blurted out the words; but they popped out before she could stop them.

'Yes, I am,' growled the man in question, pushing back a lock of jet black hair which had fallen over his brow. Then, levering himself to his feet, he unceremoniously dragged Abigail up from the floor. 'And who might you be, and what's more to the point, why did you come charging in here like a damned hurricane?'

'I did not come in like a d. . .like a hurricane,' retorted Abigail indignantly. 'I came to help, but. . .' her voice trailed away awkwardly as she suddenly realised what an awful mess she must look. Milk was dripping from the hem of her uniform on to the floor, her cap was a sodden, crumpled heap in the corner of the kitchen; and her long blonde hair, usually so neat and in a tight bun, had come unravelled and was cascading, attractively, if rather untidily, around her shoulders.

'You look as if you need a little help yourself.' he observed drily, looking her up and down through narrowed coal-black eyes.

Abigail glared at him, her large grey eyes fringed by dark lashes sparkling angrily. There was a suspicion of a twitch in the corner of his mouth, and she could swear he was laughing at her.

'So would you, if you'd been lying in a great puddle of milk,' she snapped.

'I was,' he reminded her, 'but luckily for me, you provided a perfect cushion.' He raised his black eyebrows and suddenly gave a wickedly expressive grin. Much to her intense annoyance, Abigail found herself blushing.

'I'm sorry I pulled you over,' she could hear her voice gabbling, the wretched man was making her inexplicably nervous. 'I'm afraid I just grabbed the first thing I could when I felt myself going.'

'So I noticed,' he replied coolly, giving a wry smile as he continued, 'I've only been here a short while, but already I've ascertained that Sister Collins has a pretty short fuse. *Not* the most tolerant of women! So I for one would rather not be around when she sees the mess in this kitchen, or you for that matter!'

With that parting shot he strode out of the disaster area, leaving Abigail fuming. She stood dripping dribbles of milk on the floor, glowering at Sue Parkins, who by now was cowering in the furthest corner of the kitchen.

'I'm terribly sorry,' she whispered, 'the jug slipped out of my hands and. . .but it's not broken,' she added on a more cheerful note. 'Thank goodness the new jugs are made of plastic.'

'I suppose I should be thankful for small mercies,' said Abigail grimly. Then she looked at her uniform. 'Heavens, I do look a mess! Are there any spare uniforms in the linen cupboards? I hope we brought them over with us in the move.'

'I'll go and see,' said Sue helpfully, anxious to get away from Abigail and the kitchen.

'No,' said Abigail, fixing her with a steely eye, 'I'll go. You start mopping up this mess, and do it in double quick time. You're late with the patients' teas as it is.'

'Yes, all right,' said Sue disconsolately, taking the mop from the kitchen cupboard. She swished miserably at the puddle on the floor. 'Will you be coming back?'

Abigail's expression softened; she couldn't stay cross with Sue for long. She was a nice, well-meaning girl, but terribly clumsy. 'Yes, I'll be back to help you clear up, and do the teas as well,' she said. 'You need someone to chaperone you!'

Sue brightened visibly, and started on her mammoth task of mopping up the spilt milk.

Luckily for Abigail there was a spare uniform in the linen cupboard, even though it was much too large for her slender frame. Still, beggers can't be choosers, she thought philosophically, pulling the belt tight as she changed, and hastily made herself respectable once more.

That done, she joined Sue, and soon had the kitchen clean and tidy; at least clean enough to last until the morning cleaners came on duty the next day. Then together she and Sue wheeled the tea trolley around the small side wards, and dispensed cups of afternoon tea and biscuits.

'You'd better ask Mr Lincoln whether or not he thinks Mr Weatherspoon can have tea today,' said Sister Collins as they walked past her desk. 'He did ask Nurse Orchard for some, but I'm not certain whether he's recovered sufficiently from his laser surgery to drink tea just yet.'

'Yes, Sister,' replied Abigail, feeling slightly annoyed. Why should she have to ask Mr Lincoln? She would rather have kept out of his way. Nurse Orchard should have done it, but of course Nurse Orchard never did anything if she could possibly get out of it.

Abigail sighed. Everyone got annoyed with Penelope Orchard's lazy ways, but there was little they could do about it. She was the daughter of the senior consultant surgeon at the County General, Sir Jason Orchard, and Sister Collins never reprimanded her in any way. It really wasn't fair, but Sir Jason Orchard had tremendous power which he used ruthlessly, and Penelope had no qualms about using her father's name and postion to ease her way through life. Abigail walked along the corridor towards Mr Weatherspoon's room, leaving Sue Parkins to finish pouring out the teas. The new consultant was inside, talking to the patient who had undergone laser surgery for the removal of a tumour on the tongue, only the day before. It was a new technique to the County General, performed by Greg Lincoln with equipment he had brought over from the United States. Abigail knocked on the door, wishing she didn't have to face the new consultant so soon after their first unhappy encounter.

'Come in,' called a voice, and Abigail found herself

thinking how attractive his accent was.

'Ah, nurse,' he said as she entered. Then he turned back to his patient with a smile. 'I haven't been in England long,' he said, 'but one thing I have noticed is that most of the young women here have real English peaches and cream complexions. Perhaps it's something to do with all that milk you produce on your farm.'

Mr Weatherspoon's face lit up, and Abigail knew the doctor was trying to take his mind away from his surgical problems by talking about something he knew; he was a dairy farmer and the subject of milk was dear to his heart.

'Plenty of milk is good for you,' he said, nodding his head vigorously, 'that's why our lasses look so bonny,' He smiled at Abigail standing behind the seated form of the consultant.

'Especially if you bathe in it.' Greg Lincoln glanced back at Abigail, his dark eyes glinting with amusement at the memory.

Abigail maintained a stony silence as Mr Weatherspoon ejaculated, 'Bathe in it! That would be a terrible waste of good milk.'

'Sister Collins wondered if you thought Mr Weatherspoon could have a little tea this afternoon,' said Abigail, avoiding the dark eyes she knew were on the point of openly laughing.

'I should think that would be in order, don't you?' He turned back to his patient with a smile.

Abigail turned, and started to leave the room, but was stopped in her tracks at the sound of the consultant's voice. 'Oh, nurse,' he said.

'Yes, sir?' replied Abigail, turning back to face him.

'Be sure to use *plenty* of milk!' he said, grinning

openly this time.

'Yes sir.' Her grey eyes flashed ominously.

There was really no good reason for her to feel so annoyed—after all, she knew she must have looked pretty ridiculous lying flat on her back in a puddle of milk. But somehow his overt teasing had the effect of making her hackles rise. Added to that was the fact that for some reason she couldn't fathom, she found his presence strangely disturbing.

Back at the trolley she poured out the tea for Mr Weatherspoon, and was about to give it to Sue to take up to the room, when Penelope strolled by. Her passage down the corridor could only be described as strolling, because Penelope never hurried anywhere in case one hair on her elegantly coiffured head might by chance fall out of place.

'Take this to Mr Weatherspoon,' said Abigail, holding the cup and saucer toward Sue. 'Mr Lincoln is in with him, so do try not to spill it, or even worse, drop it on the patient!'

'I'll take it,' said Penelope, unexpectedly taking the tea from Abigail's outstretched hand. She smoothed back her immaculate hair, adding with a sultry smile. 'They tell me Mr Lincoln is quite a dish. This will be a good opportunity to meet him.'

'I haven't had time to notice whether he's dishy or not,' Abigail's voice was short, 'I've been too busy.'

'One should never be too busy to notice interesting men,' announced Penelope loftily, sauntering off down the corridor, holding the tea cup in her hand.

'At the rate she's going, it'll be stone cold by the time she gets there,' observed Sue disparagingly, watching Penelope's retreating figure. Then she added, 'I don't know how you didn't notice that Mr Lincoln was dishy, because he certainly is. He's absolutely gorgeous, and oh, his hands!' She let out a long ecstatic breath of air. 'Long, tapering fingers. Didn't you notice them when he picked you up?'

'Don't be ridiculous,' said Abigail crossly. 'How on earth could I notice his hands? I was rather preoccupied at the time!' However, as she bent her head over the tea trolley she felt her cheeks burning as she remembered his words—you provided the perfect cushion! Pity he didn't meet me in a slightly more glamorous light, she reflected wryly, but common sense told her there was no point in dwelling on that!

It was almost as if Sue had been reading her thoughts, because she said with a sigh, 'It's a pity really. I think you're much prettier than Penelope, but he didn't see you in a very good light, did he? I mean when you were all dripping in milk.'

Abigail raised her head. 'And whose fault was that?' she snapped. Then she smiled as a conscience-stricken look flitted across Sue's face. 'Don't worry, I'm not out to impress our new consultant from across the Atlantic. I'm engaged already—remember? And I don't collect scalps like Penelope.' She smiled at the still worried-looking Sue. 'Come on, let's start collecting the cups now. I'm off duty at five tonight, and I'd like to be on time for once!'

As they collected the empty cups from the patients and took the trolley back to the ward kitchen, Abigail wondered about their new consultant. If he wasn't married, Penelope would certainly set out to ensnare him, although she'd probably do that even if he was, Abigail reflected a trifle cynically. It was a cynicism born of experience. As far as Penelope was concerned, anything in trousers, who was reasonably attractive, and who she considered to be on a par with her as far as social status went, was fair game. Her main preoccupation in life was men, and Abigail often wondered why she had ever bothered to take up nursing at all. She had so little interest in it.

However, once Abigail had escaped the stuffy confines of the new wards, and started the drive home, she soon forgot all about Penelope, the new consultant, and everything else to do with the County General.

It was a beautiful early summer's evening, and the plan was to go out for a meal in a riverside pub with her fiancé Rupert Blair. He had been her fiancé for six months now, a quiet steady young man, whom Abigail loved dearly, if not exactly passionately. Passionate romance existed only between the pages of romantic novels, she told herself. She was much more content with the way things really were; their relationship meandering along in a comfortable sort of way, and would end eventually in marriage, when they were both ready.

All her nursing friends who had met Rupert thought Abigail quite mad not to snap him up and marry him immediately. But for some reason she couldn't define, even to herself, Abigail wanted to wait; and Rupert never pressed her to set a date. It was a tacit agreement between them that they would know when the time came.

Shampooing her hair vigorously in readiness for the evening ahead, she thought of Rupert, and a gentle smile curved her generous lips. She couldn't understand why her friends wanted her to be so impatient, she was quite happy with things as they stood.

She had known Rupert for about two years. He was an ambitious young solicitor, and she'd met him after her father's death when he had helped her through the legal jungle of settling her father's estate. Now, she lived on alone in the ancient flint stone cottage she had once shared with her widowed father; the cottage, in fact, was the only thing about which she and Rupert had nearly come to blows.

Rupert was continually telling her that she couldn't afford to stay there, that the roof needed fixing badly, and that she should sell it; but Abigail was stubborn. She had promised her father she would stay on in the cottage. It was where he and her mother had first set up home, and for her it was the last tenuous link she now had left with a happy past.

The cottage itself was in a small village a few miles outside the town, a low two-storey building in the middle of a rambling, old-fashioned garden, filled with traditional flowers, lupins, marigolds, hollyhocks and roses. Roses, roses everywhere, at the moment overgrown and covered with sweet-smelling blooms, their scent pervading in every room in the stone cottage.

Rupert arrived at the appointed time to pick her up; he was always punctual. 'Good evening, Abigail,' he said in the slightly formal way he had. He came into the kitchen and suddenly whipped a bunch of bright pink roses out from behind his back.

Abigail buried her nose in the roses. 'Rupert, what a lovely surprise, but you shouldn't have. I. . .' with a laugh she looked almost apologetically towards the window.

Rupert followed her gaze. 'You're right, I shouldn't

have,' he said, seeing the profusion of roses outside. 'You have more than enough to fill a whole room. But these were such a bargain, such good value for money. That was the reason I bought them.'

'It's a lovely surprise, and a lovely gesture,' said Abigail, kissing him on the cheek. 'I can never have too many roses.' She smiled at Rupert's description of the roses as a bargain, he always believed in getting value for money.

As she arranged the roses quickly in a cut glass bowl, she couldn't help thinking, just a little wistfully, how nice it would have been to have had them delivered, a card with a romantic message attached. But just as quickly as the unbidden thought came, she chided herself for being so ungrateful; she was, she reminded herself, luckier than most girls to have a steady and reliable fiancé, even if he did lack imagination sometimes.

Having arranged the roses they left to go. It was an exceptionally warm June evening, and Abigail had chosen a simple cotton dress in pale sea-green. It hung loosely on her fine-boned figure, and emphasised the smallness of her waist. Her long blonde hair had been brushed until it shone like spun gold, and she had left it loose, a shimmering curtain brushing on her shoulders.

'Take a wrap,' said Rupert practically. 'You know what an English summer can be like. It may not be as warm as this when we come back.'

'I have it already,' replied Abigail, flinging a coral-coloured shawl over her arm, and trying to keep the faint note of irritation out of her voice. He meant well, she knew, but Rupert was inclined to treat her sometimes as if she'd been born with only half a brain!

Their destination was a small riverside pub and restaurant called The Tickled Trout, standing on the edge of a broad, slow-flowing chalk river, which meandered its way through a lush green vallery. This was trout and salmon fishing country, and that evening everything was serene, save for the mayflies dancing their frantic dance above the river, unheedingly skimming down to the mirror-smooth surface of the water. Every now and then there was a faint splash, as one of their number was snapped up by a hungry fish, leaping up from the green depths of the river.

Once they were settled at their table, Abigail smiled and slowly stretched. 'Bliss', she said to Rupert. 'It's been a perfectly awful day at the hospital. Moving into our new ward was bad enough in this heat, but having to put up with Sister's bad temper to boot was just too much!'

'Was she bad-tempered for any special reason?' asked Rupert as he scanned the menu.

'Well, she had good reason, I suppose,' answered Abigail, pulling a face at the memory. 'The office she'd set her heart on had been commandeered by our pushy new American Consultant.'

'Good evening, Nurse Pointer,' said a voice from the vicinity immediately behind her.

Abigail felt her face flushing a deep crimson, and her heart flipped guiltily. It couldn't be. . .yes, it was! It was Greg Lincoln, standing right by her side, accompanied by a very smug looking Penelope Orchard. Nervously Abigail raised her expressive grey eyes to his. Had he overheard? The expression in his dark eyes was impenetrable, although there was a glimmer of something—was it annoyance? she wondered anxiously, at the same time surreptitiously crossing her fingers beneath the tablecloth, and praying that he hadn't overheard her remark 'pushy new American consultant'.

But his next words confirmed that he had. 'I'm sorry I've given you the impression of being a "pushy American". You'll have to teach me some of your impeccable English manners!'

Another hot flush stained Abigail's face. Why had the wretched man to turn up at The Tickled Trout of all places? And to overhear her unfortunate remark into the bargain.

'I'm just showing Greg a little bit of the real England,' said Penelope coyly smiling at Abigail and Rupert; although she reserved the most dazzling smile for Rupert.

Good heavens, Abigail couldn't help thinking with something akin to amazement as she watched Penelope flirt with Rupert, you're not content with one man, you have to try to seduce every male in sight!

'I hope you enjoy your meal,' she said shortly, inclining her head, but not getting up. She hoped they would pass by quickly to another table.

'Aren't you going to introduce us?' asked Penelope, looking at Rupert.

Abigail felt herself getting annoyed; it was not that she felt the slightest bit possessive about Rupert, there was no need. But the way Penelope was making a play for him, while she was standing holding on to the arm of her escort for the evening, was blatant to say the least. She glanced across at Rupert. He didn't seem to mind at all. and was smiling broadly.

Suddenly Abigail saw him in a new light. Perhaps

she'd taken him too much for granted. Now looking at him through another woman's eyes, she realised that his height, and blond good looks accentuated by a slight tan, made him look rather distinguished, and dressed as he was in a navy blazer, striped shirt, tie and dark grey flannels, he had an unmistakably aristocratic English appearance.

By contrast, Greg Lincoln was wearing denims and a cream checked shirt, wide open at the neck, showing a mass of dark wiry hair curling at the base of his throat. He looked rugged and very masculine, in comparison to Rupert's cool good looks.

'Abigail?' queried Penelope again, and Abigail suddenly realised she had been surveying the two men in silence. For how long? She wondered, slightly embarrassed at her apparent rudeness.

'Oh!' She jumped up, feeling unexpectedly flustered. 'Penelope, this is Rupert, this is Penelope, and Mr Lincoln, he's our. . .'

'Pushy new American consultant,' interrupted Greg's amused voice. 'Just call me Greg.' He reached a dark muscled arm across the table to shake Rupert's hand. Abigail found herself staring with fascination at the curling dark hairs on his arm; he seemed to literally ooze masculinity in a most disturbing way. She shivered, glad that Rupert didn't have that effect on her.

Rupert laughed as he shook Greg's hand. 'Don't take any notice of Abigail,' he said, 'her bark is much worse than her bite.'

'Really?' came the reply. 'I'm looking forward to getting to know you better, Abigail.'

It was with difficulty that Abigail forced herself to look coolly into his dark brown eyes; he was laughing at her again, and she found it extraordinarily disturbing. But it wasn't the laughter that disturbed her. As her gaze was caught by his, she felt as if he had ensnared it, and that she was unable to look away. For a few short moments it seemed to Abigail that they were completely alone, that no one else existed in the room. Although cross with herself for even allowing such ridiculous thoughts to enter her head, nevertheless she found she was unable to lower her eyes.

Greg broke the moment. He looked back to Rupert, and in doing so severed the invisible bond that had been holding her gaze. 'We'd better leave you two to get on with your meal,' he said, smiling easily. 'Bon appétit.'

'Thanks, same to you.' Rupert inclined his head to Penelope first, then Greg, and sat down. 'Seems a nice enough fellow,' he said, as they passed on by to another table well out of earshot. 'She seems a nice girl too.'

Abigail snorted derisively. 'You don't know Penelope Orchard,' she said.

'Penelope Orchard,' said Rupert slowly, turning his head to look after her retreating back with interest. 'Is that the daughter of Sir Jason Orchard? I've heard of him.'

'Who hasn't?' snapped Abigail, who was beginning to wish they'd chosen somewhere else to eat that evening.

'Honestly, Abigail,' reprimanded Rupert gently, 'I've never known you to be so snappy! I'm only trying to make pleasant conversation. As far as Sir Jason is concerned, I mentioned that I'd heard of him because I might be doing some work for him soon. One of his big business ventures!'

'Sorry,' answered Abigail contritely, knowing she had snapped his head off quite unnecessarily. 'It's been one of those days. Penelope's not bad, it's just that. . .well, she's not one of my favourite people. Sorry I bit your head off.'

Rupert smiled, and reaching across the table squeezed her hand. 'Don't worry about it. Let's choose something to eat.'

They had a delicious meal, but somehow the whole evening was spoiled for Abigail. She was acutely conscious that both Greg and Penelope were continually looking in their direction, and wondered if Rupert had noticed as well.

She was quite relieved when after they had finished Rupert had suggested that they return to her cottage for coffee. 'I'll get my wrap,' she murmured hastily, ignoring the couple watching them across the room.

Picking it up, she had flung it around her shoulders and was standing waiting for Rupert to pay the bill, when to her horror she heard him saying, 'Why don't we invite Penelope and Greg to join us for coffee? They've just finished too.' He couldn't have noticed Abigail's disapproving expression, as he carried on blithely, 'It would be a nice gesture, don't you think?'

Before she could stop him, he went across to the table where Greg and Penelope were sitting, and that was that. He had invited them back, and there was nothing she could do about it without looking extremely churlish.

However, as they drove back to the cottage, with Greg and Penelope following in Penelope's car, she did say, 'I do think you might have asked me first, Rupert. I don't particularly want them back for coffee.'

Rupert glanced at her briefly, a surprised expression on his face. 'You're not usually so anti-social. I thought it would be a friendly gesture, I didn't realise you'd object.'

Abigail moved uncomfortably in her seat. He was right. Although she couldn't help thinking a little uncharitably that Rupert had probably thought it would be a good idea to get to know Penelope because of her father. Business and social life did tend to go hand in hand quite often where Rupert was concerned. She bit her lip in vexation. That was the second unkind thing she'd thought about Rupert that evening. What was the matter with her?

She sighed, feeling suddenly miserable. 'I'm sorry, Rupert, I know I'm difficult sometimes.'

Rupert chuckled and reached for her hand in the darkness. He was not in the least perturbed. 'I don't mind. I'm the patient kind, you should know that by now.'

'I do,' Abigail told him. 'and I'm glad.' She grinned, her good humour coming to the rescue. 'I suppose I'd better be nice to that wretched American,'

Rupert turned his head briefly. 'I know he's at a disadvantage not being English, but the way you say the word "American" makes it sound positively criminal!'

Abigail threw back her head and laughed, for the first time that evening 'Does it really? Poor man — all right, I'll be nice to him. Even though he doesn't deserve it!'

And not for the first time that day, she wished that her first encounter with the man in question had been in slightly more dignified circumstances.

CHAPTER TWO

'THIS IS my idea of a perfect English cottage and garden,' remarked the tall American quietly, as he watched Abigail prepare the coffee in her tiny kitchen. They were alone, Penelope and Rupert were chatting in the lounge.

'Is this your first visit to England?' asked Abigail politely, at the same time carefully setting out the cups. His dark gaze was having a disastrous effect on her, making her all fingers and thumbs, and as a result she spilt the sugar in the tray. 'Damn,' she muttered softly.

'Here, let me.' Swiftly he reached over and took the sugar bowl from her. With his other hand he grasped her wrist and pulled her hand away from the tray. 'You're almost as bad as Nurse Parkins,' he said with a smile.

Involuntarily Abigail snatched her hand away. Trust him to remind her of their first encounter!

He laughed, misinterpreting her gesture. 'I'm not going to bite,' he said gently. 'I know I have this reputation for being—what was it you said?' he paused, his glance holding an amused challenge.

'Oh . . . I can't remember,' muttered Abigail uncomfortably, remembering only too well. She made to move away from him towards the cupboard for more sugar to refill the bowl.

'Oh, I do,' he said, grasping her slim wrist again, this time even more firmly in his strong hand. 'Pushy American, wasn't it?' He laughed softly. 'Well, surely I'm not so pushy that you have to recoil from me as if I'm

23

deadly poison!'

'Don't be ridiculous,' she answered, forcing herself to look him straight in the eyes. 'I was just going to get the the sugar, not recoiling, as you so absurdly put it.' She tried to laugh causally, not with any great success, and firmly removed his hand. 'You're as bad as Rupert. He pratically accused me of being racist—he said the way I said the word Amercian made it sound positively criminal!'

Greg laughed loudly. 'Very astute of him—but then he must be,' he added with a mischievous grin, 'to have chosen you as a companion for the evening.'

'Flattery will get you nowhere,' retorted Abigail lightly, glad to steer the conversation away from the reminder of her unfortunate remark. 'Anyway, Rupert and I are engaged. I've known him for years.' She tossed him a damp cloth. 'Here catch this, it will do for wiping up the spilled sugar.' Greg caught the cloth deftly, and dutifully started to clear up the sugar. 'You still haven't told me whether or not this is your first visit to England,' Abigail continued.

'My second,' he replied, 'but the first time, I was very much a tourist. I came over when I was a medical student, for six weeks one summer with my folks. But I made my mind up there and then that one day I'd come back for longer, and really get to know England. So here I am.' He spread his hands wide in an expansive gesture, at the same time showering sugar from the cloth on to the floor. 'And I'll be grateful for any friendly overtures from the natives!' The last remark was accompanied by an expressive quirk of his dark brows.

'This native is going to be positively unfriendly, if you insist on throwing sugar all over the kitchen floor!'

Laughing at his surprised expression, Abigail snatched the cloth from his hand and threw it in the sink. Then, removing the bowl of pink roses, she proceeded to wipe the kitchen table clean of the offending sugar with a soft duster.

'Sorry for making even more mess,' said Greg, not sounding in the slightest bit penitent. Then abruptly he changed the subject. 'Lovely roses—a present from an ardent admirer?'

'No, from Rupert,' answered Abigail quickly without thinking. As soon as the words were out she could have bitten off her tongue, realising that by her remark she had implied that Rupert was not an ardent admirer.

'Ah, yes—your fiancé,' he observed. It seemed to Abigail that his voice held a questioning note to it, her *faux pas* had not gone unnoticed.

'You can take the tray in for me,' anything to get him out of the way, 'and ask Rupert to get the mints from the cupboard. He knows where they are.'

'Good as done,' replied Greg, obediently carrying the tray through from the kitchen into the lounge.

Abigail stood, coffee pot in hand, watching his retreating figure squeezing through the narrow doorway. What was it about him that set her on edge? She was normally such a self-assured girl; she had never met anyone who had disturbed her in quite the way Greg Lincoln did. It was most irritating to find herself reacting like a jittery schoolgirl; and it had all started with Sue Parkins and that wretched spilt milk. For a mature young woman, you're being ridiculous, she told herself, and picking up the coffee pot, marched purposefully into the lounge to join the others.

After serving coffee and mints, she took one for herself

and seated herself on a small stool beside Rupert, sipping her coffee and letting the conversation wash over her head. Penelope was in full flood, laughing and talking non-stop, fluttering her long lashes at both men, flirting outrageously. She *is* pretty, thought Abigail without malice, watching Penelope's animated face.

She glanced at Rupert. He was listening intently to every word Penelope uttered. For a split second Abigail felt a little pang of jealousy, then repressed it; after all, what had she to worry about? Rupert was much too sensible to go running off with another girl just because she fluttered her eyelashes. It was Greg Lincoln who would probably be taken in by Penelope, not kind, sensible Rupert.

She smiled inwardly. Yes, Mr self-assured Greg Lincoln would be the one in for a shock. Penelope had a very nasty habit of picking up males she fancied, only to drop them abruptly, when her mood changed, or something better hove into sight.

Instinctively Abigail rested her arm on Rupert's knee, in an almost protective gesture, and smiled up at him. As she did so she became aware again of Greg's dark, moody eyes staring at her. She had been so immersed in her own thoughts that for a few moments she had completely forgotten that he was sitting so close, and suddenly she knew he had been watching her face all the time.

Hastily getting to her feet, she waved the coffee pot, asking at the same time, 'Any more coffee, anyone?'

'No thanks, not for me,' said Rupert, also standing. 'I must be going. I've got an early start in the morning, nearly as early as you, Abigail.' He gave her an affectionate kiss on the cheek as he spoke.

'Yes, seven-thirty until five in the evening,' said Abigail, sighing at the thought of the long shift of duty. 'I just hope it's not as hot as today—those new wards are like greenhouses.'

'Yes, I noticed that,' said Greg, also rising ready to leave. 'I spoke to the Hospital Administrator today and told him I want blinds up by next week. The patients can't be expected to tolerate such discomfort.'

Penelope giggled and linked her arm through his. 'I bet the Hospital Administrator bowed to your command,' she purred.

'He did, as a matter of fact,' said Greg, 'but not because I commanded, but because I pointed out the salient factors to him in a perfectly reasonable way.'

And in such a way that he couldn't refuse, thought Abigail, suppressing a smile. He was commanding as Penelope had said, in a deceptively quiet, relaxed sort of way — as Sister Collins had already found out to her cost!

'Well, for my part,' said Penelope gaily, 'I don't care about the patients. I hope it's absolutely scorching tomorrow as it's my day off, and I want to sunbathe and get a tan.'

'You already have a lovely tan,' observed Rupert, escorting her towards the front door of the cottage.

'Oh, I got that in Zante at Easter,' said Penelope casually. 'Daddy and I popped over for a few days. It was absolute heaven. Mummy was already there. We have this darling little villa—you really must come over some time.'

Abigail didn't hear Rupert's murmured reply as they left the room. 'You go first,' she said to Greg, 'and mind your head on the beam.'

Greg ducked just in time. 'This house wasn't built for people like me,' he observed wryly. 'Thanks for warning me. The first people who lived here must have been very small.'

'Oh, they were. Two hundred years ago people were much smaller than we are, because of poor nutrition and other factors.'

'Yes I know,' replied Greg dryly, 'I studied human development at med school.'

Abigail flushed. She had only been trying to make polite conversation. She didn't need him to remind her *he* was the doctor!

'Yes, of course,' she replied icily

'Look, I didn't mean...' he began, but Abigail wasn't in the mood for listening, and quickly strode ahead into the tiny hall, joining Rupert and Penelope in the brick porch of the cottage.

'Thanks for the coffee.' Rupert gave Abigail a quick peck on the cheek. Then he turned to Penelope and Greg, who had joined them by this time, and extended his hand. 'Goodbye, I hope we meet you both again quite soon.'

'Oh, so do I,' said Penelope, flashing him one of her most brilliant smiles. 'We must make it a firm date.'

'Goodbye,' said Greg, shaking Rupert's hand, and then extending his hand to Abigail. 'Goodbye until tomorrow.'

Some inner devil of obstinacy egged Abigail on to ignore his proffered hand. 'Goodbye,' she replied, contenting herself with a casual wave of the hand.

Later that night, unable to sleep, she sat at her bedroom window; the perfume of roses drifted up from the garden, the aroma strong and heady on the warm night air. The familar perfume washed over her, and she relaxed, closing her eyes; but immediately her mind wandered back to thoughts of Greg Lincoln. What was it about him? Why was he so disturbing? Opening her eyes suddenly, she stared out into the darkness, at the same time giving herself a mental shake. It was illogical, she hardly knew the man, so how could his mere presence possibly disturb her? Keep your imagination under control, she told herself crossly, otherwise you'll become as paranoid as Sister Collins! Not a happy prospect, she reflected ruefully, as she finally climbed into bed and prepared for sleep. But in spite of her good intentions, Mr Lincoln's lean, dark face, with the lock of jet black hair that continually fell forward, was the last conscious image in her mind before she fell asleep.

Next morning dawned hot and humid, and Abigail groaned as she staggered out of bed and showered at six a.m. It was going to be another scorcher, that was obvious, and she didn't relish the thought of being incarcerated in the stuffy wards of the new block all day. Still, she sighed resignedly, I'm not the only one, but I do hope Sue Parkins doesn't create too much havoc today!

Of course, she should have known that was too much to hope for; she'd hardly had time to stow her handbag away in her locker before Sue's plaintive, 'something has gone wrong', voice was crying, 'Staff, are you there?'

'Yes,' groaned Abigail, wondering what disaster had overtaken the student nurse so early in the morning.

'It's Mr Jones—he's too heavy.' Sue Parkins poked her curly head around the corner of the staff room door, her face scarlet with anxiety.

Abigail laughed. 'Whatever are you talking about? I know he's a big man, but...'

'He's too heavy for the new bedpans, he's flattened it!' Sue entered the locker room, and posed dramatically in the doorway, waiting for Abigail's reaction.

'What on earth do you mean, *flattened* it? He can't have...oh no! You didn't—you couldn't have! *Poor man!*'

Abigail sped down the corridor, towards the four-bedded room where the unfortunate Mr Jones was esconced, Sue Parkins scuttling anxiously along behind her.

'But, Staff,' panted Sue, trying to keep up with Abigail, 'what do you mean? Have I done something wrong?'

'I think I know what you've done. Have you used these disposable bedpans before?'

'No,' said Sue, 'and I must say I didn't think they looked very strong. I thought when I gave it to him that it looked like some sort of egg-box!'

By this time they had arrived at Mr Jones' room, and parting the cubicle curtains quickly, Abigail went in, Sue following closely on her heels.

The Mr Jones in question was sitting up in bed, red-faced, and very embarrassed. On top of his bed was the mangled remains of a disposable bedpan. 'Ah, nurse,' he said with a sigh of relief at the sight of Abigail, 'do you think you could get me another one, a strong one? And please hurry—I'm getting desperate!'

'Of course,' said Abigail matter-of-factly, quickly picking up the offending object. 'We'll get you another right away.' She motioned with her head for Sue to leave the cubicle with her, restraining an almost overwhelming urge to giggle.

As soon as they were outside she rounded on the unfortunate Sue. 'Honestly, Sue, you really are an idiot! You should have used the rigid blue plastic rim that fixes over the top.' She grabbed hold of Sue's arm and started to propel her towards the dirty utility room. 'Just thank your lucky stars it was me that happened to be around, and not Sister Collins.'

'But I didn't know!' wailed Sue. 'Nobody told me, and I was in a hurry and I thought...'

'That's precisely what you did *not* do,' cut in Abigail, 'and really, Sue, if you're going to succeed at nursing you've just got to use some of the grey matter that's lodged between your ears. Although sometimes I do seriously wonder if there is any!'

Sue sniffed full of remorse. 'I do try,' she said plaintively, 'but it's just that I panic, and I'm always in such a rush, and then everything goes wrong and...Oh, crumbs, look who's coming!'

Automatically Abigail thrust the mangled remains of the bed pan behind her back as Sister Collins and Greg Lincoln came towards them, down the long corridor.

'You go ahead, get another bedpan, but for heaven's sake put the plastic rim on it this time, and then get back to Mr Jones before he bursts,' muttered Abigail, her mind racing ahead; she had to do something to keep Student Nurse Parkins from starting off yet another day with a black mark. 'I'll keep the evidence out of sight, and parry the opposition, should it prove necessary.'

'Thanks, Staff,' breathed Sue, 'you're a brick'.

As Sue hurried on ahead, Abigail kept walking at a steady pace, keeping her fingers mentally crossed and hoping that Sister Collins and Greg Lincoln would pass by without comment.

'Oh, Staff,' Sister Collins' voice, always slightly shrill, sounded even shriller that morning to Abigail's apprehensive ears, 'would you come with me to my office? There's a new admission, and I want to go through her notes with you.'

'Er...yes, Sister. I'll just pop along to the dirty utility room first, I promised a patient in room fourteen that I'd get a bedpan. I'd better do that first.'

Keeping the mangled bedpan clasped tightly behind her,

Abigail adopted a crabwise walk and tried to edge past both of them; out of the corner of her eye she could see Greg Lincoln watching her with astonishment written all over his face.

'Now, Staff,' said Sister Collins irritably. 'Student Nurse Parkins can do that.'

'But she...' Abigail stalled desperately as Sue dashed past with the bedpan for Mr Jones, 'is already dealing with another patient. I think I'd better do it myself, you know she can't be rushed.' Without waiting for a reply, she continued her crabwise scuttle and shot past at great speed, whipping the offending bedpan round to the front the moment she was past.

Once inside the utility room she flung the wretched article into the sluice and clamped down the heavy lid, sighing with relief as she did so; then she made her way back up the corridor towards Sister's desk. It hadn't been a particularly auspicious start to the day; she had been uncomfortably aware that Greg had been regarding her with puzzled amusement as she had made her excuses to Sister Collins. The notion that he probably thought her behaviour strange didn't please her at all; she'd wanted to appear coolly efficient. But so far all she had succeeded in doing was making herself look ridiculous; and all because Nurse Parkins was a walking disaster! It was like being on the edge of Krakotoa, working with that girl, she reflected ruefully. Life was completely unpredictable, one never knew when the next catastrophe was about to happen!

Sister Collins wasn't at her desk at the nurse's station, so Abigail went to her office and after briefly knocking, opened the door; promptly cannoning straight into the new consultant, who was on his way, and in a hurry.

'Oh dear, I'm sorry,' said Abigail politely, stepping to

one side. 'I should have knocked louder, I didn't realise you were right by the door.' 'She smiled in a friendly fashion, genuinely sorry she had crashed into him.

Her friendly smile was wasted, however, as he didn't reply, just paused momentarily to glower at her, every fibre of his being emanating hostility. Abigail stared back in surprise. She hadn't intentionally collided with him, and she had apologised, so surely there was no need for him to look quite so bad-tempered.

'Shut the door, Staff,' snapped Sister Collins in a voice rasping with anger.

Oh dear, it's going to be one of those awful days! thought Abigail dejectedly. Sister Collins will be looking for faults, and with Sue Parkins around she won't have much difficulty in finding them! As for Greg Lincoln, just a moment ago in the corridor he had looked quite approachable, but as he had walked out of the office it was quite obvious that his mood was as black as thunder.

'Fifteen minutes, that's all,' the sound of Sister Collins' voice interrupted Abigail's gloomy thoughts, and she dragged her wandering attention back to Sister Collins, who was looking at her expectantly, obviously anticipating a comment of some sort.

'Fifteen minutes?' queried Abigail, wishing she had been paying more attention.

'Fifteen minutes before Mr Lincoln does his ward round.' Sister Collins' brown boot-button eyes gleamed brightly with anger. 'I've told Mr Lincoln that *none* of the other ENT consultants here do a formal ward round, our ward is not run in that way. But would he listen?' She slapped a pile of patients' notes angrily into Abigail's hands. 'Of course not. He wants to do everything the way he did it in America. He'll be lenient today, he says, if the pathology reports aren't back, or the patients properly prepared, but tomorrow,' she waved an irate finger at Abigail, 'everything has got to he *hunky-dory.*'

'*Hunky-dory?*' Abigail's voice rose in disbelief. It was hardly Sister Collins' usual turn of phrase!

'His expression, not mine,' snapped Sister Collins bad-temperedly. She shot a glare in Abigail's bemused direction; she was still standing holding the armful of notes. 'Well, don't just stand there. Return the notes to the patients' clipboards, and get the ward ready for the inspection.'

'You remember we're one down today,' ventured Abigail, wondering if they should ask to temporarily borrow another nurse from the next ward. 'Staff Nurse Orchard has a day's leave, and we haven't made arrangements to replace her.'

'All the more reason then for not wasting time,' came the rapped reply.

All the more reason for getting ourselves organised, thought Abigail rebelliously, knowing full well it would have been only too easy for the workload to be eased, if only Sister Collins would ask for a little help. But admitting that help was needed was not in Sister's make-up. She hated admitting, even to herself, that her ward might sometimes be anything less than perfect!

Abigail began to feel bad-tempered herself, as she sped around the ward on her various tasks; I wouldn't like to end up like Sister, she thought, an embittered old woman, who can't wait to leave the hospital, and who can't bear to have the comfortable routine she's built up disturbed in any way. Then just as quickly, her bad temper changed to pity. At least her own future was rosy, she was marrying Rupert.

To Abigail's intense relief, Sue managed the rest of the whole morning without one more catastrophe. Even the ward round had gone relatively smoothly, although the atmosphere between Greg Lincoln and Sister Collins had been so intense that Abigail felt it would have been possible to slice through it with a knife! As for herself, she had kept in the background as much as possible; they were both so prickly it seemed the most politic thing to do.

'I like ward rounds,' Sue Parkins had informed her when it was over. 'It made me feel like a proper nurse, just like the ones you see in films or on television.'

Abigail chuckled. 'Just try and be a "proper" nurse for an hour while I go down to the canteen for lunch. If you need a hand, Staff Nurse Bloom on section five will help, or there's always Sister Collins.'

'No, thanks, I'll stick with Staff Nurse Bloom,' said Sue, pulling a face. 'Sister Collins is as prickly as a hedgehog today.'

'You can say that again.' echoed Abigail with feeling, as she hurried towards the nurses' staff room to get her handbag.

Once in the crowded canteen, she collected a salad and a glass of orange juice from the cold counter, then searched through the crowded tables, looking for a familiar face.

'Hey, Abigail,' it was Lynne, her friend from X-Ray Outpatients, 'I'm glad I've seen you, it saves me a phone call. Come on, let's eat outside on the terrace, I can see a vacant table.'

Together they made their way outside, on to the large terrace attached to the side of the canteen. The County General was built on a hill, and a projecting terrace had been constructed outside the main canteen. On warm summer days, the huge glass windows were slid back, and tables and chairs, shaded by gaily coloured umbrellas, put outside. It gave the place quite a continental atmosphere, and was immensely appreciated by all the staff, making it a popular and relaxed meeting place at lunchtimes.

Abigail felt the tensions draining away as she basked in the pleasant warmth of the sun; there was a cooling breeze and the umbrellas provided soothing shade.

'Now,' said Lynne, coming straight to the point in her usual fashion, 'are you coming to our barbecue next week? We're having it in the usual place, Beechwood at Hintersfield, and I could do with someone to help me with the cooking—at the moment it's only me. Is Rupert coming too?'

This speech was delivered in one breath, with Lynne demolishing her salad at the same time. It made Abigail feel quite breathless; Lynne always did.

She sipped her orange juice slowly. 'Honestly, Lynne, I don't know how it is that you don't suffer from chronic indigestion!'

'I do,' grinned Lynne, devouring a lettuce leaf rapidly, 'but come on, Abigail, I want an answer. Are you coming or not? We've got a good crowd coming as usual.'

'I'd forgotten about it,' confessed Abigail.

'Forgotten about it!' echoed Lynne feigning mock horror. 'Abigail, how can you forget the social event of the year?'

Abigail laughed. 'Sorry. The answer is yes, of course, and I'll probably bring Rupert. I'll let you know definitely by tomorrow.'

Lynne nodded. 'That will be fine, time for me to get the food sorted out. Luckily for me I won't have anything else to do this year—our new senior registrar, Derek Thompson, is a great organiser; he's hiring a portable

generator and some fairy lights, and he's doing the music.'
She suddenly smiled, 'He's awful nice, Abigail, and so go-
ahead.'

Abigail opened her grey eyes wide and grinned at
Lynne's expression. 'Don't tell me my career girl friend
has finally succumbed?'

'Not yet, unfortunately,' said Lynne, pulling a
mischievous face, 'but as soon as he gives me the
opportunity I shall succumb immediately!'

'Lynne!' Abigail tried to look severe, but only
succeeded in giggling. 'You are the absolute limit.'

'Now don't forget,' said Lynne, leaning confidentially
across the table, 'when you come to the barbecue, please
take every opportunity you get to make sure that you tell
Derek Thompson how nice I am. Clever, sexy—you know
the sort of thing. Say something that will make him notice
me.'

'Don't tell me he hasn't noticed you yet,' said Abigail
disbelievingly, 'I should have thought, working in the
same department, he would have found it impossible not
to!'

'Oh yes, he's noticed, but not in the right way, if you
know what I mean...' Lynne broke off, suddenly grabbing
her friend's arm. 'There he is now—come on!' She leaped
up from the table, dragging Abigail with her. 'We'll take
our trays back, he's making for the dirty crocks hatch too,
if I time it right we can have coffee together.'

She left Abigail no alternative but to follow, although
she would have preferred a slightly more leisurely lunch;
but at the same time she was curious to find out what it
was about the new senior registrar that Lynne found so
fascinating.

She noticed that Lynne manoeuvred herself beautifully,

so that she put her tray down on the moving belt at exactly the right moment, just in front of the senior registrar. 'Oh, sorry, Derek,' Lynne laughed gaily, sounding surprised, 'didn't see you there.'

Abigail hid an amused smile. She hadn't realised her friend was such an accomplished actress.

'Oh, by the way, Derek, this is a friend of mine, Abigail Pointer. She's a staff nurse on the ENT ward at the moment.'

Derek Thompson turned, and Abigail was astonished to find herself looking into the friendly face of a shortish, dark-haired young man, with a round face and glasses. From Lynne's ecstatic description, she had been expecting a Gregory Peck lookalike, at the very least!

'Hi,' he said, giving Abigail a shy smile.

As she nodded back a friendly acknowledgement, Abigail suddenly became aware of Greg Lincoln looming from nowhere to stand at Derek's side. His dark, lean face, with its stern expression, was a complete contrast to Derek's round, cheerful one. His expression didn't look much friendlier than it had done on the morning's ward round, she noticed, feeling inexplicably disgruntled.

'Will you join us for coffee?' she heard Derek asking them both.

Lynne nodded enthusiastically. That *had*, after all, been the whole object of the exercise, as far as she was concerned.

'Please count me out,' said Abigail politely. It was obvious Greg and Derek were together, and she didn't feel inclined to sit and have coffee with a man whose black mood of the morning was evidently still lingering.

'Why not?' asked Lynne with embarrassing directness.

'Oh, I...I've got to take some books back to the library,

now's my only chance,' lied Abigail hastily.

'What a pity,' cut in Greg silkily. 'I could do with some cheering up. It's been a bad morning.'

'I *know*,' answered Abigail pointedly, 'We've all had a bad morning!' She was tempted to add, thanks to you, but restrained herself. She also ignored the friendly expression that had flitted across his face as he had spoken.

If you think, Mr Lincoln, she thought grimly, that I'm an impressionable young thing who's going to leap joyously whenever you feel like turning on the charm, you can think again!

'I'll ring you tomorrow about the barbecue,' she said in an undertone to Lynne, then she left the trio, studiously avoiding the quizzical stare of the new surgeon. Plenty of time to see you again when you're stalking around the ward on your high horse, she thought crossly, firmly suppressing the annoying little voice at the back of her mind urging her to stay, to find out more about the American surgeon. Why should I want to find out anything more? she answered herself back. I know quite enough already!

CHAPTER THREE

THE REST of the day passed by fairly uneventfully, or as uneventfully as any day could with Student Nurse Parkins on the ward. But even she, apart from tipping, luckily a lukewarm, cup of tea into the bed of one unfortunate patient, managed to do everything more or less correctly.

Greg Lincoln didn't put in an appearance again, and Abigail could see from Sister Collins' smug smile that she felt she had scored a personal victory. She obviously thought that she put him off, the way she did all the other consultants.

'I don't think we shall be inconvenienced by a ward round again, Staff,' she said starchily to Abigail, who was helping her update the Kardex system. 'I think Mr Lincoln now knows where I stand on *that* matter. There's no need to do things the American way here.'

And I think I know exactly where Mr Lincoln stands on the matter, thought Abigail, with a feeling of foreboding. She could foresee the power struggle that was inevitable; Sister Collins had bullied all the other consultants into accepting her ways, which personally Abigail had never thought particularly good, although she'd never been in a position to voice her thoughts.

Sister Collins' main aim in life was to get by with the minimum of trouble, and Abigail had always put it down to the fact that she was near to retirement, and just couldn't be bothered. Although that was no excuse for the medical staff, who Abigail had always felt should have put up more of a fight. But they'd always opted for the easy way out.

Greg Lincoln, however, was a completely different kettle of fish; there was no chance of him taking the easy option! Abigail mentally prepared herself for the forthcoming fireworks, resolving to come in a little earlier the next day, just to make sure that everything on the ward was shipshape and spotlessly in order. She might as well do what she could to smooth what was obviously going to be a stormy passage in all their lives.

'Don't you agree, my dear?' asked Sister Collins again.

'What?' asked Abigail hastily, as she was caught daydreaming again. 'Agree with what?'

'That we won't be seeing Mr Lincoln on one of his regimental ward rounds again.'

'Well...er I...' muttered Abigail, frantically searching for something tactful to say, knowing instinctively that Sister Collins was not ready to swallow the bitter pill of reality.

'Oh, Mr Lincoln's going to do a ward round every day he's here.' interrupted Sue Parkins blithely. She'd been standing to one side listening to the conversation.

Abigail looked up quickly, trying to give her a warning glance that would tell her to shut up. But in vain. Sue carried on, blissfully unaware of the stormclouds gathering on Sister's brow

'I know', she said in a confidential tone, because I asked him. And he said that in all the hospitals he's worked in, consultants *always* did a ward round, and he's going to do one here. He's going to haul us all up by our bootstraps!'

Oh goodness, thought Abigail in exasperation, why can't that girl keep her mouth closed! Bad enough telling Sister that he's going to do a round every day, but then to imply that the ward is so badly run that it needs hauling up by it's bootstraps!

'*Haul us up by our bootstraps!*' Sister Collins' voice, always high, spiralled practically an octave until it squeaked.

'Yes, he...' Suddenly the import of her words sank in, and Sue's mouth dropped open with dismay.

'I think I heard the buzzer from room number three,' Abigail fibbed quickly. 'The light can't be working. You'd better go and see what Mrs Smith wants, Nurse Parkins.'

'Yes, Staff, right away, Staff,' said Sue breathlessly, taking the opportunity to beat a hasty retreat. She flashed Abigail a grateful look as she disappeared, realising that she'd been extricated from yet another difficult situation.

'Oh, Sister, this Kardex seems to be in a awful mess, shall I re-do it?' asked Abigail. The Kardex in question didn't warrant re-doing, but she quickly waved it vaguely under Sister's nose, hoping she wouldn't inspect it too closely. 'I'll go and get the patients' notes, and start to do it now before I go off duty.' Without waiting for a response, Abigail also made good her escape.

The very last thing she wanted was to take sides. She didn't want to hurt Sister's feelings, but in her heart she knew Greg was quite justified in his remarks. It was with a sigh of relief that she saw the night girl come on duty; time to go, and she hadn't needed to speak to Sister again. She was already in her office, packing her bags ready for departure.

'Had a good day?' asked the staff nurse coming to take over for the evening.

'Could have been better,' said Abigail briefly, not stopping to elaborate. 'Has Sister already briefed you on the patients?'

'Yes, thanks,' the night nurse grinned. 'I was briefed in two shakes of a lamb's tail, to coin a phrase! I might be mistaken, but it seemed to me she couldn't get out of here quickly enough.'

'Well, there's not much happening,' said Abigail, feeling she had to explain Sister's behaviour. 'No patients back from theatre today, as they were day cases.'

The staff nurse, whose name was Joan, laughed and sounded relieved. 'Good perhaps I'll be able to put my feet up for a bit; I've been up to London for a couple of days, and I'm absolutely shattered.'

'You shouldn't lead such a hectic life,' said Abigail, grinning. 'I've no sympathy for you. Don't work too hard,' she threw the remark over her shoulder as she too scooted down the corridor, towards freedom and fresh air. She didn't usually look forward to the end of her working day, but it seemed that ever since the new consultant had arrived, by the end of the day there was nothing she wanted more than to escape.

She rang Rupert that evening and reminded him about the barbecue the following week. They made arrangements to meet at the site, as Rupert would have to drive straight there from London.

'Oh, I'd forgotten about your London trip,' exclaimed Abigail when he'd told her. Suddenly the weekend stretched ahead, lonely and empty. 'I'll miss you,' she said truthfully.

To her disappointment Rupert didn't say anything about missing her, his head was much too full of the plans he had for all the people he had to meet. As he told Abigail, he was at a crucial point in his career, and meeting the right people now made the difference between being moderately successful, and very successful.

All he said as he rang off was, 'Be good this weekend,'

To which Abigail replied a trifle disconsolately, 'The chance to be anything else would be a fine thing!'

The prospect of the weekend stretching ahead didn't exactly fill her with delight, and she acknowledged with a feeling of slight surprise that since her father's death, she had come to depend on Rupert for companionship far more than she realised. I really ought to have more friends outside of hospital, she thought, but that was easier said than done. Working in a busy hospital, didn't leave much time for meeting people outside the world of medicine, and she was lucky to have met Rupert. Most of her friends were from the hospital, but conflicting duties often made it difficult to meet up outside the confines of the hospital; Lynne for example, she knew, was on duty for the whole weekend.

Suddenly she found herself wondering what the new consultant would be doing on his first weekend, although whatever it was he was very welcome to do it alone, or with Penelope Orchard, she reflected, pulling a face. Yes, almost certainly Penelope would invite him to meet her famous daddy!

As she prepared her supper in the kitchen she reprimanded herself for thinking such uncharitable thoughts, telling herself that if she wasn't careful she'd end up as a cross between Penelope and Sister Collins, a horrifying prospect! I shall do the garden she told herself firmly. That will stop me moping about; there's plenty to be done, the roses are running riot all over the place.

So when Friday afternoon came and the forecasters promised fine weather for the weekend, Abigail was pleased. Hard work would drive any thoughts of loneliness from her mind.

Mr Lincoln had been operating all that day, so they had been spared the rigours of a ward round, which by now had been established as a regular feature of most days. Although Abigail privately doubted whether Sister Collins would ever come to regard it as a regular feature of *her* day; it still seemed to take her by surprise every time it occured.

After waiting until Sister had gone off for tea, Abigail sneaked a quick phone call to Lynne, to confirm that both she and Rupert would be at the barbecue.

'Good,' said Lynne, then when she heard Abigail would be arriving alone, 'I'll pick you up, and you can help me get things started. OK?'

'As if I had any choice,' remarked Abigail wryly.

She glanced at her watch. Sister Collins' figure appeared at the end of the corridor and there was only about half an hour to go before off duty; but Abigail frowned anxiously. The last patient on the operating list hadn't yet returned to the ward. It was a child, having laser surgery for recurring laryngeal polyps. Normally the children went back to section five, but as this particular boy was one of Greg Lincoln's special laser cases, he was going to be nursed post-operatively on section four, where most of his beds were situated.

Abigail looked at her watch again. Should she remind Sister Collins, who was busily preparing to leave for the weekend? Eventually deciding she'd better mention it, in case it had slipped her mind that they were missing one patient, she walked over to the desk.

'Steven Brown isn't back from theatre yet,' she said. 'He went down at half past two, scheduled for theatre at three o'clock. Shall I ring Recovery and find out when he'll be returning to the ward?'

Sister Collins snorted with annoyance. 'I thought all the patients were back,' she said crossly. 'I particularly wanted to get off on time today, I'm due to catch the six o' clock train to London.' She shut the drawer of the wooden desk noisily. 'That's the trouble with all this new-fangled laser surgery, the machinery's always going wrong and causing hold-ups.'

Abigail said nothing, although she did think Sister Collins was being a little unfair. After all, they didn't know the reason for the delay, it could be nothing whatsoever to do with the laser machine.

She started to dial the number for Theatre Recovery, but halfway through put down the phone. Through the clear glass of the firedoors at the far end of the corridor she could see a trolley being wheeled along by the two theatre porters. The anaesthetist was there too, wheeling a drip stand, followed by Greg Lincoln; they were all still wearing their theatre greens.

'They're coming,' she said quickly.

Sister Collins looked up, and seeing the entourage clicked her tongue derively. 'There, what did I say—problems! That child wouldn't be needing a drip unless there'd been problems.' She bustled forward, heaving a sigh. 'This means I'll have to miss my train. I can't possibly leave intil he's settled.'

'I'll stay,' volunteered Abigail. 'It's probably something I can handle, and then you needn't miss your train.'

She went forward with Sister to meet the retinue of people coming down the corridor. 'The bed opposite the nursing station is ready,' she said, walking beside the surgeon and anaesthetist. 'Sister and I were wondering what had happened to you.'

'Well you might wonder,' said Bryn Hill, the anaesthetist, grimly. He looked pale, and still had on his theatre cap with his face mask pulled down so that it hung loosely around his neck. Abigail noticed with concern that beads of perspiration were standing out on his forehead—obviously all had not gone smoothly.

It was with gentle care that the team manoeuvred the small boy from the trolley on to the bed. The anaesthetist checked him over again, pulse, blood pressure, response to verbal commands. He left nothing to chance, and finally turned back to Greg standing at his side.

'I'm happy to leave him now, Greg,' he said, ripping off his theatre cap in a tired gesture, 'but a nurse must stay with him for the next two hours at the very least; his level of consciousness must be monitored very closely until he's back to normal.'

'That's a problem,' interrupted Sister Collins. 'We don't have enough night staff to warrant the use of one nurse exclusively to one patient. If he needs that kind of attention, he should really be looked after in the intensive care unit, where there's a ratio of one to one.'

'I know, Sister,' muttered the anaesthetist apologetically. 'But unfortunately the intensive care unit is full, and anyway I'm quite certain this boy will be perfectly all right now. It's just that I'd be happier if someone could keep a close eye on him for a couple of hours.'

'I'll stay,' said Abigail quickly. 'I've nothing special planned for this evening, so it's not a problem.'

'I'd be very grateful to you,' said Greg, speaking for the first time. 'I'm sure Dr Hill is right; there's nothing to worry about, but we don't want to take any chances with the little fellow.'

So Abigail stayed on behind when the rest of the day nurses and Sister Collins went off for the weekend; it transpired that the small boy had developed a severe tachycardia during the operation, so severe in fact that the operation had been halted. However, eventually the laryngeal polyps had been successfully lasered away, thus ensuring that his respiratory problems were resolved.

Abigail looked at Steven, lying so still in the bed, his breathing regular and peaceful now. She felt his pulse — quite normal. The parents had been in to see him briefly, and Greg had explained what had happened and then sent them away for a meal in the hospital canteen. He had promised them he would come back and meet them in an hour, so that they could see their son, and then go away reassured for the night.

Abigail smiled to herself. The new surgeon might be difficult to work with sometimes, but he was a different person with patients and patients' relatives. He had been so gentle and kind when he had been explaining to the worried mother and father, and Abigail knew that if he promised to come back in an hour, he would keep his promise. Not something that could be said for all hospital doctors, who with the best will in the world tended to promise things, but then rush off and do something else, forgetting all about their promises. Sometimes they kept patients and relatives waiting for hours; a thoughtlessness which always annoyed Abigail.

True to his word, Greg came back with the parents, and by the time they arrived young Steven was awake and demanding a drink. Abigail was just letting him have a sip of iced water when they arrived.

Greg smiled, his dark eyes crinkling at the edges with pleasure at the sight of his patient sitting up. He came to the side of the bed. 'That's much better,' he said. 'How are you feeling, young man?'

'All right,' croaked Steven. 'I'd like something to eat.'

'There's some icecream in the ward kitchen,' said Abigail. 'Shall I get him some?'

'Thank you, nurse, an excellent idea.' His sudden flashing smile had Abigail smiling back at him before she even had time to think.

Steven smiled too, at the prospect of his icecream, but Abigail hardly noticed. She was too busy trying to control the ridiculous sense of warmth that had flooded through her, all because the dark man opposite her had flashed her a sudden smile. For goodness' sake, stop reacting like a gauche teenager! she scolded herself as she hurried towards the tiny kitchen.

Once Stephen had eaten his icecream, Greg let the parents settle him down for the night, then escorted them from the ward, reassuring them that all would now be well. Abigail stayed on for another hour, just to make certain that all really was well. Having satisfied herself that Steven was well and truly asleep, she left the ward; pausing for a moment at the nurses' station where Joan was sitting writing.

'All's quiet now,' she said, 'and I'm going home.'

Joan smiled gratefully. 'Thanks so much for staying,' she said. 'I felt happier too having you with him. The only other alternative was to put an auxiliary with him. Most of them are extremely good, but unfortunately we have Nurse Dowling on tonight.'

Abigail laughed, 'Say no more,' she said. Nurse Dowling was the night equivalent of Sue Parkins, a walking disaster zone. A situation made worse by the very fact that at night there were many fewer nurses on duty, so her opportunity to create havoc was even greater than that of Sue's. 'I hope for your sake the rest of the night is peaceful,' she said.

Once out of the hospital she made her way through the hospital grounds towards her little car. She suddenly felt very tired and hot; inside the hospital it had been hot and airless, but outside seemed equally hot. Abigail felt drained, the long day and the heat taking their toll.

Unlocking the car door, she heard the distant rumble of thunder; almost simultaneously large spots of rain began to splatter down from a rapidly darkening sky. A dismal start to the weekend, thought Abigail morosely, turning the key in the ignition. The engine coughed in an unresponsive way.

'Start, please, please!' she muttered under her breath, trying again. The engine spluttered half-heartedly, then remained stubbornly lifeless.

'Oh no!' she groaned out loud. 'Don't fail me now! Not when I'm late and it's pouring with rain!' Crossing her fingers, she said a little prayer and tried again, but exactly the same thing happened. Just what I need, she thought in despair, leaning her head on the steering wheel—a car that won't go.

'Sounds to me as if you need a lift.' Greg's voice startled her. The now lashing rain had completely drowned the sound of his approaching footsteps.

CHAPTER FOUR

HE WAS standing outside the car, the full fury of the thunderstorm lashing down around him. Droplets of water flicked over her as he stuck his head through the car window.

'You're getting wet,' said Abigail, somewhat needlessly.

'I know that,' he replied, opening the car door. 'Lock up and come on. And for goodness hurry before I get completely drowned!'

In the circumstances it seemed the most sensible thing to do, and Abigail did as he commanded and scrambled into his large estate car. Once inside she turned towards him. He really was very wet; water was running down from his dark hair in little rivulets on to his face, and to make matters worse he was minus a jacket, so his shirt was completely soaked through, the wet cotton clinging to his tall, muscular frame.

In the close confines of the car Abigail was uncomfortable aware of the aura of his presence, and turned her head swiftly to look out of the window. But even as she did so, she found she was mentally comparing Rupert's fair skinned arms to the dark sinewy arms so close to hers. Rupert is completely different, she chided herself, there's no comparison, you're being unfair to him to even think about such a thing. But it was very difficult to ignore the musky smell of Greg's aftershave because it permeated the interior of the car; it caused a faint, almost imperceptible prickle of apprehension to run down her spine, and

51

instinctively she moved away.

'It's very good of you to offer, but there's no need for you to take me home,' she protested, suddenly wishing she hadn't accepted his invitation. 'I can easily get a taxi, and come back for my car in the morning.'

'Nonsense,' said Greg firmly, starting the engine of the large car. 'I'm soaking wet, and you're pretty damp. It's no trouble to take you.' He turned towards her, and suddenly flashed a devastating smile in her direction, causing her heart to skip several beats. 'Anyway,' he continued, 'it's my way of saying thank you for staying with Steven Brown.'

Abigail made no reply, as he turned the car and drove out of the hospital grounds, the rain now coming down in sheets, turning the dust of the past few days into muddy puddles. The peals of thunder seemed to get louder with every successive rumble.

Taking advantage of hs concentration on the road, Abigail sneaked a sideways glance and covertly studied his face. His dark hair seemed to have an unruly life of its own, she noticed, the heavy forelock always falling forward, even now when it was wet. His rugged face with its determined and somehow slighly sensual mouth was attractively tanned; indicating that he must spend as much time as possible in the open air. Probably to make up for having to work on stuffy wards, and the even more claustrophobic confines of the operating theatre, thought Abigail. Perhaps he was aware that she was studying him, for he turned again suddenly, flashing her that same heart-stopping smile.

Nervously she flashed a brief smile back at him, then looked hastily away, discomfited at being caught staring. 'You must be careful not to miss the turning,' she said hurriedly, 'otherwise you'll end up going miles out of your way.'

'And that would never do, would it?' he replied, laughter lurking in the depths of his voice. Abigail knew that he had seen her discomfiture, and was amused; it had the effect of making her feel even more disconcerted, and she wished yet again she had refused the offer of a lift.

At last they reached the gate of her cottage, the roses around the gate bowing their heads as if in sorrow at the fierce onslaught of the storm. Greg pulled the car to a halt.

'Are you going to ask me in?' he asked abruptly.

The abruptness of the question startled her, she hadn't even thought about it, for a moment she hesitated. Then common sense took over. After all, it was merely of matter of courtesy to do so.

'Of course, you can dry yourself off a little. Perhaps by then the storm will have abated.'

'It certainly hasn't at the moment,' he observed, adding as he looked at the length of the garden path. 'We're going to get quite a bit wetter by the time we reach the cottage.'

Abigail nodded in agreement, and then together they ran the whole length of the path as fast as skirting the deep puddles would allow. Even so, it was impossible to avoid being completely drenched all over again, by the time they reached the shelter of the brick porch.

Exhausted from running, Abigail inserted the key into the lock and pushed open the front door. 'Well, at least we're in the dry now,' she said breathlessly, 'and to think I'd planned to do some gardening tonight!'

'Is that *all* you'd planned to do?' asked Greg teasingly.

Abigail blushed, and was immediately annoyed with herself. Any other man's teasing wouldn't have caused her to react like a sixth-form schoolgirl! What was the matter with her?

'Rupert's away until Wednesday,' she heard herself blurting out defensively, 'and I...er' ...Her voice trailed off, as she found herself studiously concentrating on a button in the middle of his shirt. 'You're *very* wet,' she finished lamely.

'I could say the same about you.' His voice seemed extra low and husky, or was it her over-active imagination?

Abigail looked up quickly, but then tried to look away again as she caught a disturbing glance from his enigmatic coal-dark eyes. But his hand caught at her chin, determinedly tilting her face back towards him.

For a brief moment, she resisted pushing her slender hands against the warm wetness of his soaked shirt. Then the persuasiveness of his mouth on hers melted her resistance, causing strange unknown emotions to stir within her, spreading through her veins with a warm glow.

'Put your arms around my neck,' he commanded, his lips warm against her cheek.

Meekly Abigail slid her willing arms around his neck. The pressure of his long sensitive fingers against her body was strong, and long-dormant emotions she hadn't even known she possessed instinctively made her raise her face to drink in his deepening kiss. Fleetingly, Rupert's face flashed before her, but she couldn't retain it. Greg's dark face was there, warm and close, blotting out everything and everyone else.

At last he drew back his head and smiled gently down at her. 'Do you like me a little better now?' he asked slowly. 'Or do you still regard me as that "pushy" American?'

Abigail felt her cheeks staining pink with embarassment, as she realised the interpretation he was probably placing on her response to his kiss. 'I'd better get you that towel I promised,' she muttered quickly, evading a reply to his question.

He laughed softly, a faint hint of mocking amusement in his laughter. 'Is that a way of telling me to stop?'

With the relative safety of two yards now separating them Abigail felt more confident, 'Yes, and it's also a way of telling you that if we don't both dry ourselves we shall catch pneumonia.' With that, she skipped smartly up the stairs not waiting for his reply. Hurriedly grabbing two warm bath towels from the airing cupboard, she leaned over the banister and threw one down to him.

'Catch!' she called. 'Dry yourself as best you can, I'll be down in a moment.'

Having thrown down one towel, she dashed into her bedroom, immediately going over to the mirror to peer anxiously at herself. Wonderingly she touched her lips, the lips Greg Lincoln has just a moment ago kissed so thoroughly.

What was she going to do? She should never have let him kiss her, she realised that, of course.

'He caught you by surprise,' she whispered out loud, trying to excuse herself. But that was no reason to respond in such an abandoned manner! her conscience reminded her. What about Rupert. . . yes, what *about* Rupert? Why was it that his kisses didn't have the same effect? It was a question she couldn't answer, and she felt miserably confused. Usually cool-headed and in complete command of her emotions, she felt uncertain and hesitant, unsure of what to do next.

Briskly towelling herself dry, she changed into a T-shirt and jeans. Keep cool, she advised herself firmly, and don't let him get too close! After all, you can't exactly blame him if he's drawn certain conclusions, you didn't exactly give him the old heave-ho!

Eventually, firmly suppressing all her nerves, she marched purposefully down the stairs, with an outward show of confidence; keeping her fingers crossed that she would be able to keep the charade for the duration of Greg's stay.

She found him in the kitchen. He had taken off his shirt and laid it across the hot water boiler. 'Do you mind?' he asked matter-of-factly. 'It's thin cotton, and should only take a few minutes to dry.'

'Oh, no. . .of course not,' said Abigail, as casually as being faced with an enormous, half naked man in her kitchen would allow! 'Are you sure you won't be cold?' she added. 'I'm sure I could find a sweater to fit you,' she finished in a rush.

'I don't need a sweater,' replied Greg, not in the least embarrassed. 'But I wouldn't say no to a drink or something to eat.'

She hadn't been expecting him to invite himself to supper, but rose to the occasion nevertheless. 'How about some wine and pizza?' she asked quickly. 'I've got some in the deep-freeze, they won't take long to cook.'

'Sounds great' said Greg, adding with a grin. 'I was beginning to think you were going to throw me back out into the rain, because you still didn't like me!'

'Of course I like you, silly,' said Abigail lightly, determined to keep the conversation at a lightly bantering level. She delved into the depths of the deep-freeze, searching for the pizzas. 'And even if I didn't, it would be very ungracious of me to throw you back into the night, especially as you rescued me and brought me home.'

'Ah yes,' said Greg, raising his eyebrows in his customary manner, 'those impeccable English manners of yours. I was forgetting those.' Then he added softly, so softly it was almost inaudible, 'I was thinking that perhaps you regretted kissing me,'

'No, I don't regret it,' said Abigail carefully, forcing a casual smile to her lips as she turned to him, 'but of course, I never place too much importance on a little thing like a kiss! Do you?'

'No, of course not,' agreed Greg, a strange quizzical look lurking at the back of his eyes, 'but then I hadn't realised quite what a woman of the world you obviously are.'

'Oh, there'a a great deal you don't know about me,' said Abigail gaily. 'A woman of the world'—oh, if only he knew just how dull she really was!

'Here catch,' she threw two frozen pizzas at him, which he caught deftly. It broke the tension, and they both laughed. 'We ought to open a bottle of Italian wine,' said Abigail turning to the little wine rack she kept in the corner of the kitchen. 'What would you like, Orvieto or Chianti?'

'Chianti,' replied Greg, without a moment's hesitation. 'I have some Italian relatives living in Tuscany, so Chianti is my favourite.'

Abigail handed him the bottle to open and took the pizzas from him, placing them in the oven. 'I've never been to Italy,' she said wistfully. 'Perhaps one day I'll go, when I've paid for all the repairs needed for the cottage.'

Greg's gaze flickered over her with a questioning expression for a moment, but he made no comment other than to tell her that Italy was a magic place. His voice had taken on a soft note when he had spoken. 'Magic,' he said, 'almost as magic as England.'

'Oh, I was beginning to think you preferred America,' said Abigail without thinking.

'Whatever gave you that idea?' He sounded surprised,

Then he smiled, twisting his lips into a lobsided grin. 'Is it because of the ward rounds?'

'Well, yes, I suppose it is partly that,' admitted Abigail. 'You do seem to like to do everything the American way.'

'I like to do everything the *best* way,' he said firmly. 'It's immaterial to me whether it's the English or American way, just as long as it's the best.' He looked at her through narrowed eyes. 'Do you object to the ward round too?'

Abigail burst out laughing at his look of concern. He looked genuinely hurt, 'No, of course I don't, I happen to think it's good medical practice, and it's a pity our other consultants don't do it. But I can't help feeling sorry for Sister Collins, it isn't easy for her to change her ways.' Glancing across, she saw a stubborn look settle on his face. 'You could try being a little bit nicer to her,' she ventured. 'It would help to make all our lives more pleasant.'

'It's the patients' lives I'm concerned with,' said Greg uncompromisingly, as he uncorked the Chianti bottle, 'not Sister Collins' complexes, or anyone else's, for that matter.'

Abigail bit her lip angrily. It was a snub. She had only been making a friendly suggestion, something she was surely entitled to do? He was, as she had observed before, one moment friendly, the next distant and aloof. But she held her tongue, although she couldn't resist giving him an angry glower out of the corner of her eye as she went across to the oven to check on the pizzas.

As she opened the oven door, she was suddenly aware that he was standing very close behind her. 'I've said something to annoy you again,' he said.

Abigail didn't answer, she was far too conscious of his nearness, too conscious of the ridiculous hammering of her own heart. Her hand on the oven door handle trembled, as slowly he placed his large hand over hers and pushed the door shut. Without releasing her hand, he turned her slowly round to face him. But a flickering tinge of fear made her stiffen, as she reminded herself that she was engaged to Rupert, and she was *not* the woman of the world Greg Lincoln thought her to be.

Greg responded immediately to her faint movement of withdrawal. 'Abigail?' his voice was questioning.

'I'm engaged to Rupert, I don't want to. . .' her voice faltered, it sounded hypocritical after the way she had responded to his previous embrace.

He laughed softly and the sound unexpectedly tore at her heartstrings. 'OK,' was all he said. Then he tipped her face up to his, smiling quizzically at her flushed features. 'On reflection,' he continued, 'I think perhaps I'm hungry for that pizza now, it smells delicious.' Turning away from her, he picked up his shirt, completely dry by now, and pulled it over his head.

To Abigail's immense surprise and relief, the rest of the evening passed in easy conversation. She had expected to feel shy and awkward with him, but soon found they had plenty to talk about. She forgot her initial shyness as Greg told her about himself and his family. She learned that his mother was Italian and his father an American dentist, just about to retire; they planned to spend at least half the year in Italy, Greg told her. His sister was the same age as herself, and a successful model in New York. From his affectionate anecdotes about his family, Abigail could tell they were very close, and found herself envying him.

'I hope you'll be able to meet my parents soon,' said Greg as he polished off his pizza. 'I shall take a vacation with them in Italy. You could always visit—they love visitors'.

Abigail just smiled. The chances of her taking a holiday in Italy were zero, she reflected wryly; the upkeep of the cottage saw to that! Instead, she told him about her father, and how she still missed him; how she had never known her mother very well because she had died when she was a small child.

Don't you have any other family?' asked Greg.

'No one, 'said Abigail, 'not unless you count a very elderly aunt who lives in Aberdeen, and I've only met her once!'

'That's sad,' said Greg slowly, looking at her with his dark eyes.

She tilted her chin proudly. 'Don't feel sorry for me,' she said defensively. 'I've got plenty of friends, and I've got Rupert.' But even as she said it, she knew she did envy Greg and his close-knit family. From what he had told her they sounded fun, especially his mother, who sounded terribly Italian, over-dramatising everything to larger-than-life portions.

'I don't feel in the least bit sorry for you,' replied Greg quickly. 'Don't be so prickly!' Then he grinned. 'What I should have said is that you've got the kind of personality that would fit in well with a large family group. I can just imagine you surrounded by hordes of children, with your hair hanging down in riotous curls. Like it was the first day I met you.'

Abigail blushed furiously at the memory. 'Thanks for the backhanded compliment!' she replied, collecting the plates and glasses from the table. 'However, I cannot imagine myself like that—I'm a career girl at heart.'

Greg pulled a disbelieving face which she ignored. Stacking the dishes in the sink, she suddenly realised how late it was. The kitchen window was open, and the warm night air wafting in was filled with the fragrant fresh perfume that always comes after summer rain.

'Time for you to go,' she said decisively, turning back towards him. 'I've got a lot to do tomorrow.'

Greg allowed himself to be ushered out without protest. He left, not attempting to kiss her goodnight, and after he had gone Abigail leaned against the solid wood of the front door, not knowing whether she was pleased or sorry!

CHAPTER FIVE

MONDAY and Tuesday of the following week passed by in a flash. The ward was busy with plenty of new admissions, and Abigail was very pleased to see dear old Mr Weatherspoon well enough to go home. He had recovered very well from his laser surgery, and Greg had told her that he was hopeful he had managed to remove all the tumour.

'His prognosis is good,' he said.

Mrs Weatherspoon had bought in a large stone jar of homemade cider when she came to collect her husband, 'Can you make sure Mr Lincoln gets this?' she asked Abigail as together they packed her husband's belongings in a suitcase 'I've told him about English cider, but I don't think he believed me when I told him how strong it was!'

Abigail laughed. Mrs Weatherspoon was looking quite concerned. 'Don't worry, I'll make sure he gets it, *and* the message. I'll warn him to drink it at home, when he has nowhere to go. He'll be sorry to miss you, I know, but he's busy operating today.'

After Mr and Mrs Weatherspoon had departed, Abigail and Sue Parkins cleaned out the room ready for the next occupant. Sister Collins had decided to keep the room temporarily empty, in case they had an emergency admission. Privately Abigail thought it was a silly idea. If they did have an emergency, the patient would need to be near the nursing station to be observed, and that would mean moving someone else into Mr Weatherspoon's old room. It would have been much better to have moved a patient now, she reasoned, when they had some spare time, rather than to leave it and have to do it when they were rushed off their feet with an emergency admission. She sighed. Sometimes Sister Collins didn't seem to use any common sense at all, in spite of all her years of nursing experience.

As it happened, when the emergency case did come in, it was the following day, just before Abigail was due to go off duty—an old lady was admitted with a chicken bone lodged in her throat.

Abigail almost felt like saying, 'I told you so,' to Sister Collins when Greg came along and told them about the patient, adding that she would need to go into the bed opposite the nursing station.

'As Mr Smith is going home tomorrow,' he said, 'he can be moved into the side room, and we can put Mrs Jewell into his bed.'

'Mr Lincoln,' Sister Collins replied icily, 'I am quite capable of organising my own ward.'

'Good,' was the only comment, before he strode off down the corridor.

Thank you very much! Abigail felt morose. He had come in, with a few words stirred up Sister Collins into a foul mood, then marched off, leaving her to bear the brunt of Sister's bad temper. But there was no time for more than a fleeting mental grumble—there was work to be done, and by the time Mr Smith had been moved, lock, stock and bedside locker; and an anxious Mrs Jewell installed in the appropriate bed, it was way past the time when Abigail should have been off duty.

Oh heavens, she thought, glancing down at her watch, Lynne will be waiting—I'll be late for the barbecue. She'd brought some jeans and a teeshirt into the hospital with her, and hastily scrambled into them in the changing room. When she finally made the frantic dash downstairs, it was to find Lynne pacing up and down impatiently in the car park.

'About time too,' was her comment, as they both jumped into Lynne's old banger, laden up to the gunwales with boxes of food and wine. 'Come on, it takes absolutely ages to get the charcoal going.'

It was a gorgeous summer's evening, a clear sky splashed with streaks of gold, the temperature warm and balmy. In spite of the temporary set-back of the storm of Friday night, the spell of good weather was holding. Lynne drove quickly, chattering non-stop all the way to the site, which was several miles out of the town, set deep in a clearing of woods belonging to the Forestry Commission. A Forest Ranger was waiting for them when they arrived, and helped them to get the fire for the barbecue started before he left.

Derek Thompson had also arrived early, and was rigging up lights strung between the trees, to be run from a small petrol-driven generator he had put behind the old barn which stood on the edge of the clearing.

'Sorry, girls,' he said as soon as he spied them, 'but I'm not going to be able to stay. Bob Raleigh has been stricken with some ghastly bug, and I've got to go back on duty.'

'Oh Derek!' wailed Lynne, her big eyes round and reproachful.

'Sorry,' said Derek, completely misunderstanding her disappointment, 'but don't worry, I've organised one of the theatre technicians to take down the lights. All you've got to do is take the generator back in your car. I'll pick it up from you tomorrow.'

'But you'll miss the barbecue,' grumbled Lynne.

'Needs must,' answered Derek, putting the finishing touches to the lighting. 'I'll come round to your place tomorrow night and pick up the generator, if that's OK, and perhaps we could go out for a drink. That is,' he added hastily, 'if you're not doing anything else.'

'Good idea. I think I'm free,' said Lynne nonchalantly.

Abigail hid a smile. She thinks she's free! She knew very well that Lynne would move heaven and earth to be free for a date with Derek Thompson; and she teased her about it when Derek had left.

'Well, I don't want to appear too keen,' said Lynne, smiling complacently, 'I might have put him off.' She laughed happily. 'Come on, we've got loads to do.'

Between them they managed to time it just right. Some senior house officers from Casualty came, and organised the drinks side of the evening, and Abigail and Lynne soon had the steaks, hamburgers, sausages and jacket potatoes cooking on the huge grill of the iron barbecue. It was hot and smoky work, but Abigail didn't mind that; she was hot and sticky and had soot streaked across her face, but she was enjoying herself. The barbecue was going with a swing, the fairy lights sparkled merrily between the trees, and muted music echoed round the forest clearing.

She was happily turning over sizzling steaks with a long prong held in one hand, and drinking red wine from a plastic beaker held in the other, when she was suddenly aware that three people were looking at her.

It was Rupert, with Penelope hanging on his arm, and standing slightly behind them, Greg Lincoln. Suddenly Abigail was aware that she was very scruffy indeed, knowing her face was flushed from the heat of the fire and the red wine, and she was also acutely conscious of the contrast between herself and Penelope, who looked coolly immaculate as usual in cream-coloured cotton slacks and a purple silk blouse.

'Abigail, what a mess you look!' laughed Rupert, confirming her worst fears. He came up and pecked her on the cheek. 'this girl never does anything by halves,' he added, turning to Greg and Penelope, still laughing.

'You must be mad, Abigail,' said Penelope, wrinkling her straight little nose in disgust. 'You'll smell smoky for a week!'

'Somebody has got to lend a hand and help out,' retorted Lynne sharply—she'd never had much time for Penelope. 'If we waited for you to volunteer, we'd wait until next year!'

'Not until next year,' corrected Penelope, giving one of her tinkling laughs, as she drifted away to talk to some acquaintances, 'for ever! Only fools volunteer for hard work!'

'It'll be a fine day when she volunteers for *any* kind of work,' said Lynne indignantly, venomously prodding a sausage.

Abigail couldn't help laughing at Lynne's outraged expression. 'It doesn't worry me,' she said truthfully, 'and Lynne, please don't treat that poor sausage as if it's Penelope Orchard!'

Lynne laughed and speared the sausage even more viciously, then mischievously waved it under Greg's nose, 'I didn't know you were coming,' she said. 'Your name wasn't on my list.'

'Derek Thompson said I could eat his share,' he replied, grinning back at her. 'Shall I give you a hand? I think you should move some of that meat now, unless you want your steaks to end up as charcoal!'

With Greg's help they piled up the cooked food to one side and left people to help themselves; the glowing embers of the fire were left to die down a little.

'Come on,' said Greg in Abigail's ear, 'I've got a plate of food for you—come and sit over here and eat it, you deserve a rest. You too,' he added to Lynne, 'you both deserve to take it easy. Rupert, can you carry Lynne's plate?'

Rupert nodded, and they followed Greg across to one of the rustic wooden picnic tables which were dotted about the site.

'This is nice,' said Lynne, while Greg went off in search of some wine for their party. 'He's thoughtful isn't he?'

'Sometimes,' replied Abigail, making a face; she was thinking of that afternoon when he'd left her to shoulder the wrath of Sister Collins!

Greg returned and they sat squashed together eating and drinking. 'It tastes really good,' remarked Abigail, tucking in with relish. 'I didn't realise how hungry I was. I could eat a horse.'

'You probably are,' joked Lynne.

Rupert laughed,' It's because of all that energy you've used up,' he said, putting an arm around Abigail's shoulder and giving her an affectionate squeeze. Then he wrinkled his nose.' Penelope was right— you do smell smoky.'

'You have no taste,' Abigail teased him. 'It's the latest perfume, "Smoke gets in your Eyes"!'

'Sorry, but I definitely prefer Chanel No 5,' said Rupert. 'Promise me you'll be wearing that next time I see you.'

'I promise,' laughed Abigail, and kissed him lightly on the side of his cheek before turning back to her barbecued supper.

It was as she turned that she was startled to catch a strange gleam in Greg's dark eyes. She was certain it was almost a kind of anger she saw glinting in the depths of his eyes. At least, she thought it was a kind of anger. But why? Why should he be angry? Puzzled, she stared back, only to find his gaze caught hers and ensnared it. Suddenly the memory of him on the night of the storm flashed before her mind's eye; she could see him sitting in her kitchen, his bronzed torso gleaming in the light of the lamp while his shirt had been drying. At the uninvited memory, an involuntary shiver ran the length of her spine, and hurriedly she looked at her plate, afraid that her agitated thoughts might be mirrored in her eyes. Precisely at that moment Penelope Orchard chose to come across to their table, and for once in her life Abigail was actually glad to see her.

'Hi, everyone,' Penelope purred throatily, sliding her elegant form down on to the wooden seat beside Rupert. 'I really must congratulate you, Lynne, you've organised a superb barbecue supper as usual, and I gather we're to have live music as well as the canned variety this year.'

Lynne looked at her watch. 'Thanks,' she said briefly, then stood up. 'I'd better ask Bruce and Dougie to start playing, we only have until half past midnight on the site.' She left them and went off to find the two guitar players.

The assembled company crowded round the fire, which had been given a new lease of life. Someone had thrown on some dry logs, and the orange flames licked hungrily at the tinder-dry bark, illuminating the faces of the crowd. Soon everyone was singing along in company with the lilting music.

In the crush Abigail lost sight of Rupert, but she didn't worry, she knew he was there somewhere and she would find him when it was time to go. She was content to sit on the sweet-smelling grass watching the faces of her friends in the flickering firelight.

'You look like a pixie sitting there with your knees hunched up under your chin.' Greg's voice at her side startled her. He sat down beside her and casually draped an arm around her shoulders. 'It's a lovely evening isn't it?' he said.

Abigail stiffened at the touch of his arm. 'Yes, it is a lovely evening,' she agreed uneasily. 'At this time of the year the weather is usually beautiful in England.'

'It wasn't the weather I had in mind,' he rejoined, his low voice and teasing. 'I was thinking how lovely it was sitting here with you.'

'Oh,' said Abigail, totally at a loss, and not knowing what to say next; unprepared for such a direct compliment.

Laughingly he pulled her closer. 'You are a puzzlement, Abigail,' he said softly. 'When I kissed you last Friday, you responded at first like a warm, passionate woman; the kind I like. But then you drew back, and made that quaint comment about being engaged to Rupert.' He laughed again.

Abigail turned her head swiftly, flashing him an angry look in the semi-darkness. 'I *am* engaged,' she answered in a low trembling voice. 'Maybe I'm old-fashioned, but I don't approve of flirting with other men'.

Greg's only comment to her angry rejoinder was, 'I'm sure Penelope Orchard isn't old-fashioned!'

Still angry, she turned her head away. 'I don't care to emulate Penelope Orchard,' she said stiffly. 'What she does is her business, and what I do is mine!' Scrambling hastily to her feet, she stood up, intending to walk away, but to her consternation he also stood up, and grasped her slim wrist in his hand, the long fingers fastening like a steel vice around her wrist.

'There's no reason to take offence,' he said, and Abigail thought she had detected an annoyed note in his voice too, then just as suddenly it disappeared as he laughed and added, 'I wasn't trying to seduce you.'

'You couldn't, even if you wanted to,' she said very deliberately. 'I can't speak from experience, as I've never been seduced, but I've always imagined that one has to be, at the very least, slightly attracted to the man concerned!'

She knew the barbed remark went home, as Greg dropped her wrist immediately; an opportunity she took to walk swiftly away. She didn't look back—she didn't need to. She knew he was standing alone on the edge of the crowd watching her, but his tall, lean figure had been swallowed up by the darkness as she approached the light of the fire. To her intense relief she soon found Rupert, who was still with Lynne and Penelope.

'Where's Greg,' asked Lynne, stifling a yawn.

'I don't know,' lied Abigail quickly, 'I haven't seen him for simply ages. He must be talking somewhere.' She waved a hand vaguely at the crowd around them, now beginning to disperse in dribs and drabs after the evening's festivities.

'You look tired,' said Rupert with concern to Lynne. 'Shall I help you pack up? It's just gone midnight.'

Lynne yawned again. 'Yes, I supposed we'd better make a start,' she said reluctantly, adding, 'The only trouble with organising is that everyone buzzes off at the end, and they never think of offering to help.'

'I'm offering,' Rupert reminded her.

Abigail linked her arm through Rupert's and smiled up

at him. 'Yes, you can always be relied upon,' she said gently.

He pulled a wry face, 'That usually means someone is dull,' he said sombrely.

'Oh Rupert, I didn't mean that,' she protested, her grey eyes serious at the thought that she might have hurt his feelings. 'You *are* reliable, and I mean it in the nicest possibly way.' Impulsively she leaned forward and kissed him warmly. It was true, she felt so safe with Rupert, a warm and comfortable affection. No frightening quivers up and down her spine, no strange feeling in the pit of her stomach, the way she'd felt when Greg had kissed her.

Putting her arm around his waist, she smiled up at him agin. 'Come on, let's start loading Lynne's car'

It was more or less as Lynne had predicted. When the evening broke up, most people went off, but a few stayed on to help, including the two musicians Bruce and Dougie. They helped Rupert dismantle the lights, the technician who was supposed to have done that having disappeared.

Abigail noticed out of the corner of her eye that Penelope had disappeared with Greg Lincoln through the darkness in the direction of the parked cars, long before everyone else had left. Have a good time with our local good-time girl, she couldn't help thinking uncharitably! But try as she might to keep them at bay, disturbing thoughts of the strength of Greg's arms insisted on creeping into her mind, coupled with an image of Penelope encircled by those same arms.

It's none of your business, she told herself firmly. You have Rupert so why even waste a single thought on a man like the new surgeon? A man who likes fast women, as he more or less told you! She pulled a rueful face as she humped a box of rubbish into Lynne's car. No, she was definitely not in the *femme fatale* class!

Almost as if to confirm her thoughts, Lynne remarked casually, 'You know, I think Greg Lincoln is a bit of a womaniser.' Then she chuckled as she climbed into her car and slammed the door. 'But he'll have met his match in our Penelope!'

'Drive safely,' was all Abigail said, as Lynne backed her battered car round in a semicircle, with complete disregard for the uneven tussocks of grass, before zooming off, accompanied by the clatter of a disintegrating exhaust, into the night.

'Do you know, that's the first thing you've said for the last half hour,' remarked Rupert. 'I was beginning to think you'd fallen asleep!'

Abigail sighed. 'I'm tired, Rupert.' It was a good excuse for her silence. She could hardly tell him that her thoughts had been occupied almost exclusively by Greg Lincoln!

As they drove back to the cottage, she let her head rest comfortably against Rupert's shoulder, and resolutely refused to let any stray thoughts of Greg Lincoln so much as creep into her mind.

When they reached the cottage, Rupert drew her gently into his arms and kissed her. Then he drew back. 'Is something wrong, Abigail?' he asked.

Abigail shook her head mutely. His kiss was warm, gentle, and undemanding. How could she say that after only one kiss from the new American surgeon she couldn't get him out of her mind? It was too ridiculous.

'I'm tired,' she said again, 'it's been a long day.'

Rupert brushed her cheek with his lips. 'You work too hard,' he said with genuine concern in his voice.

His gentleness was suddenly too much for Abigail;

inexplicable tears welled up in her eyes, and she flung herself into his arms. He was such a comfort!

'I don't know what I'd do without you,' she blurted tearfully.

Rupert's arms tightened around her. 'You don't have to do with without me,' he said. 'We can get married soon.'

It took a few seconds for his words to sink into Abigail's tired and confused brain, and when they did she drew back her head to look at him. 'Soon?' she questioned.

'Is that such a strange idea?' he asked. 'You know I love you, we're engaged, so why wait any longer?'

Abigail remained silent. She hadn't meant to precipitate the subject of marriage. She hesitated, not knowing what to say, suddenly very unsure of herself. She did love Rupert, she knew she did, she was sure she did. But marriage — that was another thing; so definite, so final. Somehow, it had always seemed such a long way off, it was something she had not bothered to think about very seriously.

'Marriage is a big step.' she said at last, very slowly, measuring out her words carefully. 'I'm not sure that I'm ready for it yet.'

'I don't mean tomorrow, or next week, silly, said Rupert with laugh. 'I mean, let's set a firm date, something we can look forward to.'

'A firm date,' stammered Abigail, suddenly feeling vaguely panic-stricken. 'Oh I don't think. . .'

'In three months,' he interrupted her swiftly. 'You can leave work then, leave the hospital. We'll go to the Caribbean for a month's honeymoon—you've always said you wanted to go there.'

Abigail looked at him uncertainly, then sense and good reason took over. It *was* a good idea, they couldn't go on putting off marriage for ever, and Rupert was so considerate. How could she be anything but happy with him? Solid, dependable Rupert.

'Yes,' she whispered tremulously, 'in three months.'

'Good girl,' said Rupert. 'I'll start making the arrangements.' He ruffled her hair. 'You are a funny girl, Abigail—you don't sound very excited. I thought girls were always ecstatic about getting married!'

'Oh I am,' she hastened to assure him, 'It's just that three months is not far away, and I'm not certain whether I can get everything done. They'll have to replace me on the ward, and. . .' She'd been about to say what about the cottage, shall we live here? But her words were lost as Rupert kissed her, taking her lips with a passion that surprised her. She let herself relax in his arms, wanting to respond, to please him, but her unruly thoughts dragged up the memory of Greg Lincoln's persuasive kiss; although she tried, she couldn't relax. Perhaps Rupert sensed her reticence, because he gently released her and kissed the tip of her nose.

'Just think, in three months' time, you'll have got rid of this old cottage,' he nodded his head in the direction of the house. Abigail opened her mouth to protest. That was the last thing she wanted to do, but before she could speak Rupert carried on happily, 'We'll be sunning ourselves in the Caribbean without a care in the world. 'Then he added, 'You *will* wear your ring now, won't you? Now that we've fixed the date.'

'Yes,' murmured Abigail, feeling, irrationally that events were rapidly becoming totally out of control. She knew Rupert; when he said he'd make all the arrangements, he would. Nothing would be left to chance. He would fix the church, the reception, everything. He was a great organiser.

It was difficult not to, but she decided not to mention the cottage. Not for the moment anyway. They always argued about it. She'd have to choose her moment, and hope to persuade Rupert that it would be a good investment to stay there.

Later that night, however, as she lay in bed thinking of Rupert and her forthcoming marriage, she felt happier. She couldn't wish for a more considerate man. He wouldn't be likely to try to seduce another man's fiancée—not like the unscrupulous Mr Lincoln!

Next day, Penelope sauntered on to the ward, late as usual, looking extremely smug and pleased with herself. Like the cat who's stolen the proverbial cream, thought Abigail in exasperation, trying not to wonder what had happened between her and Greg Lincoln the night before. The image of his dark head against Penelope's elegantly coiffured blonde hair flashed before her mind, only to be suppressed just as quickly, as she determinedly concentrated on her work.

Mrs Jewell, the emergency admission of the previous day, was needing all Abigail's concentration; the old lady was going down to theatre later in the morning to have the piece of bone removed under general anaesthetic. Abigail was getting her ready for theatre, helping her to change into the loose theatre gown, tied with strings at the back.

'I'm terribly worried, dear,' quavered the old lady apologetically.

'Worried?' asked Abigail in a reassuring tone of voice. 'There's nothing to worry about. You'll be in very good hands, Mr Lincoln is the best surgeon here, and he'll have that little piece of bone out in a jiffy. I expect you'll go home tomorrow.'

'It's not the bone I'm worried about,' confessed Mrs Jewell, 'it's my bowels.' She looked embarrassed.

Abigail smiled. It was the usual worry of elderly patients, no matter how serious their other ailments might be. 'You've been starved since yesterday,' she said gently. 'As soon as you wake up and feel able to, you can have something to eat, and then everything will sort itself out. You'll see.'

'Are you sure?' Mrs Jewell didn't sound convinced.

'Quite sure,' said Abigail firmly. Now promise me you'll stop worrying.'

'I promise,' replied Mrs Jewell uncertainly. But Abigail knew she almost inevitably would go on worrying about it, in spite of being reassured.

The theatre porters came, and Sister Collins asked Abigail to accompany Mrs Jewell down to the theatre suite. As she was handing over the notes to the theatre nurse, she caught a glimpse of the tall figure of Greg Lincoln. He was in his theatre greens, and walking through to scrub up for the next case. In spite of herself, she felt her heart lurch treacherously at the sight of him.

She knew it had been a long and busy morning's operating, and the sight of his tired face drew a reluctant pang of pity from her. He might be a womaniser, but he certainly worked hard. For his part, he seemed absorbed in his own thoughts, and didn't notice Abigail as he strode by.

Giving Mrs Jewell's hand one last reassuring squeeze, Abigail left the confines of the theatre suite and went back to the ward and Sister Collins.

'Can I have a twelve-till-one lunch hour today?' she asked 'I have to meet a friend.' She had promised Rupert she would try to meet him for lunch. He would wait for her outside the hospital. Abigail hadn't particularly wanted to go, but Rupert had insisted that they have a celebratory lunch.

'To set the final seal,' he had said.

Sister was in an unusually sunny mood and agreed at once. 'Are you planning to do anything special?' she asked.

'No, nothing special,' answered Abigail. It was true, she didn't feel it *was* anything special. A guilty little voice nagging at the back of her mind told her she ought to feel wildly elated; but it was with a strangely heavy heart that she left the ward just before twelve to meet Rupert.

The huge sliding doors at the front entrance parted silently for her to pass through, and as she walked towards the waiting Rupert, she saw to her consternation that he was not alone. He was talking to Greg Lincoln. For a moment she hung back, disconcerted. He was the last person she had expected to see; he had finished operating too soon as far as she was concerned. Irritably she glowered at the two men in her line of vision. I'm not in the mood to talk to the hospital Lothario! she thought crossly!

However, she had to be polite—he was, after all, one of the consultants to whom she was responsible. 'Hello,' she said on reaching them, 'is this a welcoming party?'

Greg answered first. 'I supposed you could say that.' His dark eyes searched her face. 'I hear I'm to congratulate you on finally deciding on the great day.'

Abigail's hackles rose. The tone of his voice expressed boredom. Fine, she thought, I don't want you to be interested, so you needn't pretend! 'Yes, that's right,' she replied frostily, then slipping her arm through Rupert's,

'Excuse us, won't you. I only have an hour for lunch.'

'You're lucky, that's a lot more that I'm going to get,' Greg observed wryly as he turned and walked back into the hospital. 'Mind you're not late back on the ward,' he threw the remark over his shoulder, as the glass doors parted and the interior of the hospital swallowed the shadow of his figure.

Abigail gasped furiously. The cheek of the man—she was never late! Rupert, however, didn't notice the subtle insult. He just smiled easily as he remarked. 'you didn't mind me telling him, did you, darling?'

'No, of course I don't mind,' muttered Abigail, 'but I don't know why you bothered. He isn't interested. All he cares about is the hospital, and that it should be run efficiently.'

But Rupert's mind had already moved on to other matters. He was looking at her left hand. 'Where's your ring?' he asked. 'I thought you were going to wear it.'

'I am,' said Abigail, pulling out a gold necklet from inside her uniform. 'I've threaded it on this.'

'Can't you wear it on your finger?'

'Well. . .' Abigail hesitated, 'yes, I can, there isn't a rule about rings on the ward.' Rupert waited expectantly, so she slipped the ring from the necklet and let him place it on the third finger of her left hand.

'It should have been there three months ago,' he remarked as he slipped it on.

Abigail looked at the big ring sparkling on her finger. It was foolish of her, she knew, there was no reason to hide the fact that she was engaged, but somehow it made her feel uncomfortable, It's because it looks rather ostentatious with my uniform, she told herself.

She was determined not to be a single minute late back

on the ward after her luncheon date; the very last thing she wanted was for Greg to be able to find any fault with her. So she was back at least five minutes earlier than necessary, and took over the nursing station from Sister Collins, who was grateful for the extra minutes it added on to her lunch break.

She was sitting at her desk, sifting through notes, when she caught a glimpse of the surgeon out of the corner of her eye; he was striding along the gleaming polished floor of the wide corridor, making straight for the nursing station. Abigail bent her head studiously, without indicating that she had seen him, and started laboriously filling in some pathology reports.

'Nice lunch?' he enquired, stopping in front of the desk.

'Yes, thank you,' said Abigail, not looking up.

'You don't look over the moon, if you don't mind my saying so,' he observed.

'I *do* mind you saying so.' Her head jerked up sharply. 'I choose not to wear my heart on my sleeve, that's all.' She shifted uncomfortably in her seat, wishing he would move away from the desk. 'It's part of my typically English reserve,' she added, tilting her oval chin at him defiantly.

Greg laughed, and Abigail bent her head low again to avoid his dark quizzical gaze. She sifted assiduously through the pathology reports, very conscious of the sparkling diamond ring on her finger.

'Quite a rock!' remarked Greg, picking up her hand to inspect the ring closer. Then he dropped her hand abruptly, saying, 'You really are old-fashioned, you obviously believe diamonds are a girl's best friend.'

Drawing in her breath sharply, Abigail opened her mouth to make a tart reply, but the opportunity was lost, as he turned on his heel and without a backward glance strode off down the corridor. She stared resentfully at his retreating back. How dared he insinuate that she was a gold-digger!

Of course it wasn't long before both Penelope and Sue noticed the cluster of diamonds sparkling on Abigail's finger.

'That must have cost the earth,' said Penelope, a note of envy in her voice. 'You are lucky. Rupert is not only good-looking, he's got breeding *and* money.'

'I thought you preferred Americans,' Abigail just couldn't resist a little dig.

'Only on a temporary basis, until something better comes along,' replied Penelope airily. She looked at the ring again. 'Why have you never worn it before?'

'I don't know,' Abigail answered truthfully. 'But now we've fixed a date, the end of September, Rupert thought I should wear it.'

'I see . . . the end of September,' was Penelope's only comment, then she appeared to lose interest.

Sue Parkins, however, was all of a twitter. 'I only hope I can find someone like your Rupert,' she said, her eyes as big as saucers. 'It's so romantic!' She sighed dramatically. 'I don't think I'll be able to concentrate on anything for the rest of the afternoon.'

'So what's new?' Abigail teased her.

Greg Lincoln came back on to the ward mid-afternoon, a string of medical students in tow. 'No need to worry, Sister,' he said, noting Sister's alarmed expression. 'This is not a ward round, just an informal visit with some second-year students.'

'Do you want a nurse to assist you—Nurse Pointer could do it?' asked Sister Collins, sounding relieved.

'Isn't Nurse Orchard free?' asked Greg, not looking in Abigail's direction, 'I thought she could help me today.'

After the entourage had disappeared down the corridor, Sister looked at Abigail, a surprised expression on her face. 'That's strange,' she said, 'he usually makes a point of asking for you.'

'Do you think perhaps there's a romance going on there?' asked Sue Parkins, leaning on Sister's desk and swinging one leg excitedly.

A sharp glance from Sister's beady eyes made her stand up straight, and pull her ruffled uniform smooth. 'I really don't know, and I'm not the slightest bit interested in anyone's life outside of this ward,' Sister Collins retorted sharply.

'She didn't even notice your ring,' whispered Sue to Abigail later. 'You'd think she'd be interested.' Then she added thoughtfully, 'I wonder what her life is like when she's off duty.'

Abigail smiled. 'I don't know, but I have the feeling she's rather lonely. Perhaps that's why she's not more cheerful.'

She was surprised, therefore, when Sister Collins came up to her that evening, just as she was about to leave.

'I hear you're to be married in September,' she said gruffly.

'Er . . . yes,' replied Abigail, feeling suddenly awkward. She twisted the ring nervously on her finger. 'You don't mind me wearing it?'

'Of course not, I hope you'll be very happy.' Sister replied. Then her expression softened. 'It's very sensible of you, my dear—get married soon, and grasp happiness while you can. It can disappear all too quickly.'

Abigail looked at her, seeing a woman different from

the one she usually saw. 'Yes, Sister,' she said.

The older woman paused a moment, smiling reflectively. 'I wasn't always a crusty old spinster,' she said. 'I was engaged once, but I was young and I wanted to wait until we had enough money for a house. It was a mistake, the house wasn't important.' She paused again, then continued quietly, 'He was a pilot. He flew on the last bombing mission of the war, and never came back . . . there isn't even a grave I can visit. Sometimes it seems as if it was all a figment of my imagination.'

Impulsively Abigail reached out and touched her arm. 'Oh, Sister Collins,' she said, her heart going out to her, 'I'm so sorry.'

Sister Collins sighed and patted Abigail's hand. 'Thank you, but it's all a long, long time ago, although the feeling of emptiness is still there. So that's why I say to you, when the right man comes along, grab him while you can.' With that, she walked briskly from the changing room, almost as if she was already regretting her confidence.

Abigail looked down at the ring winking back at her from her finger. When the right man comes along, grab him, she reflected. It was good avice, and she had got the right man. She smiled happily. Yes, Rupert was the perfect man, there was nothing to worry about.

Still smiling, she stepped into the corridor, only to bump into Greg as he made his way back to the ward. Yes, she thought again, Rupert is the right man, not like you, Mr Lincoln, who'll be going back to America at the end of the year, no doubt leaving a trail of broken hearts behind you!

He had one of his black moody expressions on his face, but undeterred, Abigail smiled sweetly. 'Goodnight, Mr Lincoln,' she said gaily, resisting the sudden impulse to wave her diamonds defiantly under his nose.

'Why the Mr Lincoln bit?' he asked, still looking bad-tempered.

'I'm feeling formal,' said Abigail, adding cheekily, 'I *am* English, you know!'

'*Don't* I know!' replied Greg sarcastically.

It was Abigail's turn to glower at his retreating back. He's had the last word as usual!

CHAPTER SIX

'COVER for me, will you?' Penelope whispered to Abigail, looking furtively up and down the corridor to see if Sister Collins was in sight. 'I've just got to nip down to Theatre, something urgent I must do.' Without waiting for Abigail's reply, she was off down the corridor. For once in her life she was actually hurrying.

Abigail suppressed a smile at the unusual sight of Penelope moving at something other than a leisurely pace. Sister Collins can even instil fear into you! she mused.

'Honestly, Staff, I don't know why you bothered to do anything for her,' hissed Sue Parkins, who had overheard. 'She's a rotten, selfish . . .'

'Ah, ah, ah!' reprimanded Abigail, wagging her finger in admonition at Sue. 'You mustn't call people names!'

'Well, she is,' replied Sue unrepentantly, 'and I know where she's gone.'

'Oh?' said Abigail absentmindedly, glancing down at the watch hanging from her uniform; it was almost time for the patients' morning coffee. 'Where has she gone, that's so important?'

'To see Greg Lincoln, of course,' said Sue. 'If you ask me, I don't think he's that keen, but she's using Daddy's influence to get him interested.' She sniffed disdainfully. 'Sir Jason is holding his annual "At Home" at the end of this week; she's just gone down to give Mr Lincoln his invitation.'

'It's coffee time,' snapped Abigail, with an unexpected

rush of irritability. 'Come on, I haven't got time to stand here gossiping, and neither have you.'

She started to walk quickly towards the ward kitchen, trying to ignore the irrational stab of resentment she had felt when Sue had imparted the gossip about Penelope. Why should you care? she asked herself, trying to be reasonable. Whatever Penelope Orchard and Greg Lincoln do is their business, not yours'?

The resolution not to even allow herself to think of them caused her to nag Sue into moving a little faster. 'Let's try to get the coffee round finished on time for once,' she said.

Sue shot her a few curious glances, thinking how unlike Abigail it was to be bad-tempered, but she said nothing. As a student nurse, and one who was always getting into scrapes, she knew better than to question her elders when they had forbidding expressions on their faces!

Penelope rejoined the ward just as they had finished, with her usual perfect timing; meeting them as they pushed the trolley laden with dirty cups, down the long corridor towards the ward kitchen.

'Oh, have I missed the coffee round?' she asked innocently, eyes wide.

'Yes,' snapped Abigail.

'You managed to time that just right,' said Sue cheekily, not surprisingly to be rewarded with a withering look from Penelope.

'I had no idea of the time,' drawled Penelope, still fixing Sue with a steely gaze, 'otherwise, *of course*, I would have come back to help. I know it's difficult for you two to manage,' she added with poisonous sweetness.

It was with great difficulty that Abigail refrained from picking up one of the wooden trays and hitting Penelope over the head. Instead she had to content herself with saying, 'Now that you're back, Penelope, perhaps you could help Sue give Mr Knott a blanket bath. He's in room three.'

Penelope sighed heavily, at the mere thought of work, but started off down the corridor. 'Get everything together, Parkins,' she said loftily, 'then we'll do him, although I must say I hate nursing that particular man. He will keep trying to talk, and I can never understand a thing he says.'

Sue flung the last tray down with a clatter on the kitchen worktop. 'Get everything together, Parkins!' she mimicked Penelope's 'plum in the mouth' accent. Then she turned to Abigail, her fresh face screwed up and pink with anger. 'Sometimes I *hate* her!'

'Sue,' Abigail sighed, 'you must get used to working with people you don't always like. I'm afraid you'll meet quite a few more Penelopes in this world.'

Sue nodded. 'I know, but that doesn't mean I have to like them.' She left the kitchen and started off towards the utility room, then suddenly backtracked and popped her head round the kitchen door. 'And *I* shall talk to Mr Knott, even if she doesn't. I think he's marvellous—lots of people give up after a laryngectomy, but he hasn't. I just know he's going to be able to talk properly one day.'

Abigail smiled at Sue's figure, as she bustled from the kitchen bristling with indignation. In spite of all her faults, she would make a good nurse one day, because she really cared about people. People like Mr Knott, struggling to learn to speak again after a laryngectomy for carcinoma. Yes, she reflected, Sue Parkins had compassion, something Penelope completely lacked.

The rest of the morning passed quickly. New admissions for Friday's operating list kept Abigail and Dr Singh, their new senior house officer, busy. It was almost time for Abigail to take her lunch hour when the telephone on the desk rang.

Sister Collins picked it up. 'Yes, yes, she's here.' She passed the phone to Abigail. 'It's for you—a personal call. Please keep it brief.' Her voice was abrupt, signalling her displeasure; she hated nurses taking personal calls on the ward.

Abigail was surprised to hear Rupert's voice at the other end of the line, he had never rung her before at the hospital. 'What's wrong?' she asked immediately, thinking something awful must have happened.

'Nothing,' replied Rupert, 'in fact everything is perfect.'

'In that case,' began Abigail, 'why . . .?'

'Because today is Wednesday and I'm not seeing you until Friday,' said Rupert, anticipating her question. 'And that's the night of Sir Jason's "At Home".'

'What on earth has that got to do with anything?' asked Abigail.

'I've been invited,' said Rupert, 'with you, of course, as you're my fiancée.' He sounded pleased. 'I've been angling after this for a long time, meeting up with Penelope has turned out to be a boon. I can probably land a very important commission with Sir Jason's influence. So it's important that we go.'

'Important for you to go,' said Abigail, pulling a face at the thought of the sort of social function she hated, 'but not surely for me? Anyway, you know that sort of thing isn't really my scene.'

'If it's important for me, then it should be for you. As my wife you'll have to get used to these sorts of things. Big business deals are usually hatched at such events.' Abigail felt a guilty pang as she heard the note of irritation in

Rupert's voice. He was right, of course—he usually was. He carried on, not waiting for her reply, 'I rang you now so that you can get your wardrobe organised. Wear something special, something glamorous.'

'Perhaps you've already decided what I should wear?' she enquired mildly but pointedly.

'Abigail darling, of course not!' Rupert sounded anxious. 'It's just that it's very important for me, and I wanted to give you plenty of notice.' He paused. 'You will come, won't you?'

Abigail smiled into the phone. Of course Rupert was just being considerate—what was the matter with her? As Rupert's fiancée she had to go. 'I'll choose something flattering, don't worry,' she said. 'See you on Friday evening.'

She put the phone down slowly, knowing she would be the envy of most of the other girls if they knew she had been invited to one of Sir Jason's 'At Homes'. She ought to be excited, but an uneasy feeling of apprehension had settled over her like a mantle. She was being irrational again, she knew that, but something inside her was telling her she ought not to go.

Friday evening duly arrived, almost before she knew it. The ward had been so busy that she hadn't much time to indulge in any worries about the forthcoming event. It had been arranged that Rupert would pick her up at seven-thirty, and as she started to change and shower, her thoughts turned to the evening ahead. Idly she wondered what the much-talked-of affair was really like. Everyone who'd ever been to one had returned in raptures—fabulous, they all said.

For Rupert's sake, she took a lot of time and trouble with her appearance. All for Rupert's sake, she told

herself firmly; the fact that Greg Lincoln would be there
had nothing whatsoever to do with it. Although she did go
so far as to admit to herself that she was glad he would be
seeing her in a more glamorous light for once, and not
scruffy as she had been at the barbecue.

Her hair was shampooed and brushed dry until it shone
like spun gold, then she slipped into a pure silk coral-
coloured trouser suit. The material clung subtly to her
softly tanned skin; it was expensive, and opulence seemed
to flow from every pleat and tuck in the material. The suit
had been a present from her father, one of the many things
he had brought back for her after one of his business trips
to Hong Kong.

It was daring and exotic, and Abigail had never worn it
before. She looked sideways at herself in the long bedroom
mirror. It suits me, she thought, but . . . At the thought of
the evening ahead, butterflies began to flutter in her
stomach. The outfit was stunningly daring, but looking at
herself Abigail knew that no one would ever guess that the
girl inside it was feeling nervous. The pants were slightly
baggy, coming in very tightly to a band at the ankles, and
the soft jacket knotted under her breasts, leaving an
enticing expanse of bare midriff; on her feet she wore a
pair of strappy gold sandals.

A second glance in the mirror almost panicked her into
changing into something plainer, more ordinary. But no,
she glowered back at her nervous reflection in the mirror,
no, for once she would look as glamorous as Penelope.
Have courage, my girl, she told herself firmly—after all,
your father bought it for you, it's about time you wore it.

Almost defiantly, she liberally sprayed herself with a
musky perfume, and then spent the last half hour before
Rupert's arrival hastily painting her nails and toenails

a delicate coral colour to match the outfit.

Rupert's mouth literally dropped open with astonishment when she answered his knock on the cottage door. 'Abigail,' he breathed, 'you look absolutely gorgeous! I shall be the envy of every man in the place!' He put his arms round her and kissed her.

Abigail kissed him back, wanting to feel something more than a comfortable sensation. But no electrifying prickles quivered their way along her spine, her body remained stubbornly unresponsive.

But her kiss satisfied Rupert, who squeezed her affectionately, and said, 'Come on, we don't want to be late.'

The house of Sir Jason and Lady Orchard was in the next village from Abigail's cottage, about fifteen minutes by road, and soon they were being ushered into the sumptuous house.

Privately, Abigail thought the green and gold marble floor, and the potted palms and statues in the entrance hall, a bit ostentatious and overwhelming. Rupert liked it, however. 'This is what it's like to have *real* money,' he enthused, looking around.

Champagne was flowing freely, and they were caught and drawn into a swirl of laughing, talking people, like two leaves floating on water. But Abigail found, in spite of her previous misgivings, that she began to enjoy herself. Rupert was relaxed and happy, and she found she was never short of someone interesting to talk to. There was no sign of Greg Lincoln, or Penelope for that matter, but then, as she looked around, she realised that was hardly surprising; the house was very large, and crammed with people.

Feeling distinctly mellow after several glasses of

champagne, Abigail was standing talking to one of Rupert's legal colleagues, when she became aware of a group of people bearing down upon them. Turning her head, she saw it was Penelope, Sir Jason and Lady Orchard, with Greg Lincoln at the rear.

'Hello, we just *had* to come over,' said Penelope archly. 'We've been socialising—one must, you know. But at last we've got to *you*, Abigail.'

She laughed, a tinkling little laugh which never failed to grate on Abigail. It always sounded so false. Penelope carried on blithely. 'I said to Daddy, we simply *must* go and find Abigail, she must be feeling so out of it!' She looked around for Rupert. 'And even your fiancé seems to have deserted you.'

'Don't worry about me, Penelope,' said Abigail politely, fixing a determined smile on her face, 'I've had a fascinating evening; and Rupert hasn't deserted me, he's over there.' She waved a hand in the direction of Rupert.

'I'm so glad you're enjoying yourself, my dear,' said Lady Orchard. 'I do so want everyone to enjoy the evening.'

'I am,' Abigail was able to assure her, as the introductions were made, and she shook hands with her host and hostess.

Sir Jason snapped his fingers imperiously at a passing waiter. 'A tray of the best champagne,' he ordered in his rich plummy voice.

Abigail didn't like him, she never had; he was an arrogant man. She had only worked with him once, in an outpatient clinic, and had noticed that he talked to all his patients as if they were imbeciles. However, there was nothing for it but to smile and make polite conversation. He was the host, and Rupert wanted to impress him, she reminded herself.

She couldn't help noticing Penelope eyeing her outfit, and allowed herself just the teeniest feeling of smug satisfaction, secure in the knowledge that every inch of her looked glamorous—quite a change from the neat, trim staff nurse usually seen on the ENT ward. She could also see Greg's dark eyes lingering in surprise, taking in every facet of her revealing trouser suit; she flashed him a suitably haughty look.

Rupert joined them, and immediately he and Sir Jason starting talking business. From the snippets of the conversation she overheard, Abigail gathered that Sir Jason had Rupert in mind for some legal transaction abroad, although what it was she had no idea.

A small orchestra started playing on the crowded terrace, and Penelope immediately dragged Greg away to dance. Abigail made polite, if somewhat stilted, conversation to Lady Orchard, who turned out to be really rather nice. Not at all like her daughter or husband, thought Abigail in surprise.

The music stopped, and Greg escorted Penelope back to the group. 'May I have your permission to have the next dance with your fiancée?' he asked Rupert.

'Oh, I don't feel like dancing,' said Abigail hastily, taking a sip of champagne to dispel the dry nervous lump that had quite suddenly appeared, threatening to suffocate her.

'Go on,' laughed Rupert, 'you can't refuse Greg. He's a friend and colleague.'

'No, you can't refuse me,' Greg echoed.

Unwillingly Abigail glided on to the dance floor with Greg's arm pressed firmly around her waist. To her surprise, they moved together well, in perfect unison.

Abigail almost pinched herself to make sure she wasn't dreaming, dancing with Greg had a trancelike quality, she felt that only the two of them existed. The tangy smell of his skin so close to her face reminded her of the night he had kissed her when his shirt had been wet from the rain.

'The last time I held you in my arms we were quite alone,' he said, reading her thoughts with an uncanny accuracy.

'We're not alone now,' she reminded him, taking care to keep her voice noncommittal, and at the same time draw herself away from the subtle pressure of his arms. 'Apart from a hundred or so other people, I'm here with my fiancé.' She put a slight pressure on his shoulder with her hand, trying to put a little distance between them.

He would have none of it. His hand, stronger than hers, pressed determinedly into the small of her back, so that he was holding her even closer. At the same time, he steered a course firmly into the middle of the now crowded dance floor, so that they were out of view of the others.

'I do believe if I kissed you right now, you'd respond in exactly the same way you did the other night,' he said, half teasing, half serious. 'I don't believe you really love Rupert Blair, I think you're marrying him for security.'

Abigail raised her head, her luminous grey eyes flashing dangerously. 'How dare you say that!' she whispered. 'That's a despicable thing to say.'

'Tell me I'm wrong, then,' he growled, 'but I don't think I'll believe you.'

She stared at him, anger beginning to rise, making her want to hit his smiling face, to hurt him physically, but fighting for control, she kept her voice coldly even as she replied. 'I don't care whether you believe me or not, Mr Lincoln. Your opinion doesn't interest me in the slightest.

Please take me back to the others, I want to stop dancing *now*!'

His answer was to hold her even tighter, until she felt she was suffocating. But although she was hating him for his cruel remarks about her forthcoming marriage, she couldn't deny that the very same thoughts had lain dormant at the back of her own mind. Wretched man! she thought furiously, trying to wrench her hand from his. He had the perfect knack of going to the very heart of the matter, and it hurt.

'Let me go,' she whispered between clenched teeth, but his answer was a brief but shattering kiss, right there in the middle of the dance floor. His impudence knew no bounds!

'Take that as my congratulation on your forthcoming marriage,' he said quickly. Abigail glanced worriedly over her shoulder, and he noticed. With a short laugh, he added curtly, 'don't worry about your precious fiancé seeing that little kiss, he's much too busy discussing business with Sir Jason.'

Abigail glared at him, her grey eyes reflecting a mixture of apprehension and anger. 'I shall take the kiss for the congratulation you said it was,' she said quietly, 'and as far as wondering about my marriage, I can tell you right now it will be successful.' Her voice sounded more confident than she felt, as with a quick twist she manoeuvred herself out of his arms. 'As I've told you before, I'm old-fashioned, and I happen to believe that marriages should last. I intend to see that mine does.'

'Huh!' Greg snorted.

But Abigail didn't give him the chance to reply, as she swiftly made her way from the crowded dance floor and joined the rest of the group. Although inwardly seething with a confusing mixture of emotions, somehow she managed to present a cool, calm appearance. But when Greg passed her another glass of champagne, with a wickedly questioning flicker in his dark eyes, she would have dearly liked to have thrown it straight at him! Instead, she had to content herself with taking it, acknowledging the glass with a gracious nod of the head.

The rest of the evening was spent with Rupert and the Orchards, Abigail all the while studiously avoiding catching Greg's eyes, although without looking in his direction, she knew he was watching her and Rupert together; his remarks echoed repeatedly, and very uncomfortably, through her head.

Rupert, of course, noticed nothing, and anyway he was very much engrossed with Sir Jason, until in the end Abigail began to wonder impatiently when they would stop talking. When he eventually did announce that he and Abigail must leave, she tried not to look too enthusiastic, although inwardly she greeted his words with a feeling of immense relief.

When at last they left, Rupert drove her straight back to the cottage. 'You weren't annoyed,' he asked, 'because I was talking business so much? But Greg seemed to do a good job of looking after you,' he added as an afterthought.

Abigail laughed, it was meant to be lighthearted, but somehow it came out strained and brittle. 'I didn't need Greg to look after me,' she said, anxiously wondering whether perhaps Rupert had seen the kiss after all, 'and of course I didn't mind—business is business. Was it something exciting?'

'It might be,' replied Rupert mysteriously. 'There might be a trip abroad in it; for both of us. How would you like that?'

'I'd love it,' said Abigail truthfully. 'Am I allowed to ask where?'

'Italy,' said Rupert, bending to kiss her a brief goodnight, 'but don't mention it to anyone yet.'

She touched him tenderly on the cheek as he left her. Dear Rupert, she loved him so, but why, oh, why didn't he set her on fire?'

Sleep eluded her that night. Greg's dark, handsome face with the quizzical smile hovered maddeningly in front of her every time she closed her eyelids. Eventually she drifted off into an uneasy sleep, but even then, that dark brooding face crept into her dreams, and she awoke in the morning still remembering the touch of his lips on hers.

To say that she felt like death warmed up the following morning was an understatement! The result of a late night, too much champagne and fitful sleep left her hollow-eyed and pale. For a moment she was almost tempted not to go in, but then forced herself to get up and go into work.

It was Sue Parkins' study day, which meant they would be one short on the ward, and she knew there were several patients due for discharge, and new ones to be admitted for operations the next day, so it would be busy. Her conscience would prick her too much if she stayed away, and as she reminded herself, it was her own stupid fault she felt so rotten; one glass of champagne too many!

As she walked on to the ward from the changing room, she firmly pushed her hair back beneath her cap, telling herself her headache was all in her imagination, there was nothing wrong with her.

Her determined effort at feeling well evidently wasn't good enough, though. Joan's first remark as Abigail approached the desk was to say, 'Goodness, Abigail, you

4 BOOKS PLUS A CLOCK AND MYSTERY GIFT

Here's a sweetheart of an offer that will put a smile on your lips . . . and **4 FREE** Mills & Boon Romances in your hands. **Plus** you'll get a digital quartz clock and a mystery gift as well.

At the same time, we'll reserve a Reader Service subscription for you. Every month you could receive 6 brand new Mills & Boon Romances by leading romantic fiction authors, delivered direct to your door. And they cost just the same as the books in the shops — postage and packing is always completely FREE. There is no obligation or commitment — you can cancel your subscription at any time. So you've nothing to lose! Simply fill in the coupon below and send this card off today.

Please send me 4 FREE Mills & Boon Romances and my FREE clock and mystery gift.

Please also reserve a Reader Service subscription for me. If I decide to subscribe, I shall receive 6 brand new Romances each month for £7.50, post and packing free. If I decide not to subscribe I shall write to you within 10 days. The free books and gifts will be mine to keep in any case.

I understand that I may cancel my subscription at any time by simply writing to you. I am over 18 years of age.

9A8T

NAME_____

ADDRESS_____

_____

_____POST CODE_____

look simply *awful*.'

'Thanks, that's all I need,' said Abigail, leaning on the desk with an air of resignation, 'and here I was trying to convince myself I felt OK!'

'Problems?' asked Joan curiously.

Abigail pulled a rueful face. 'Nothing much, just a surfeit of champagne.'

Joan laughed unsympathetically. 'Lucky thing! I've never even had the opportunity! Anyway, I thought champagne wasn't supposed to give you a headache?'

'I can tell you with absolute certainty, that story is a myth. Champagne can and does most definitely give you a splitting headache. And I'm speaking from experience!'

Joan laughed again. 'Well, you'll get no sympathy from me,' she said, collecting up her things and starting to leave. Then she paused a moment, looking at Abigail's pale face speculatively. 'My advice to you is to snatch a quick cup of coffee. There's still some left on the patients' trolley.'

Abigail took her advice, and was sitting at the nursing station sipping the coffee when Greg Lincoln came along.

'Headache?' he asked.

She could see the glint of amusement in his eyes. 'Yes,' she answered briefly.

Picking up the now empty coffee cup, she left the desk, and hurried down the corridor, catching the kitchen maids just as they were wheeling the trolley through the fire doors. She felt Greg's eyes almost literally boring holes in her back, but instead of returning to the nursing station, as she had originally intended, she made a pretext of needing to go into the utility room, waiting there until he had left the ward and gone down to his outpatient clinic.

That way, she managed to avoid him for the whole of the morning. As there was an extra large outpatient clinic

Greg had cancelled that morning's ward round, just leaving Dr Singh with a list of tasks to perform.

Mrs Jewell was discharged, and went off happily to go back home, with strict instructions to be more careful next time she was eating meat containing small bones.

'Don't worry, dear, I will,' she said to Abigail. 'I don't want to end up in hospital again.' She patted Abigail's hand. 'Everyone has been very nice to me, dear, but there's no place like home.'

As the morning wore on, so Abigail's headache gradually lessened, but she was still left feeling lacklustre and tired. Not enough sleep, I suppose, she thought wearily, wishing lunchtime would come so that she could sit down. But she was on late lunch that day, so there was nothing for it but to keep on working, and by the time she did eventually make her way downstairs to the canteen, she felt like dropping in her tracks.

Most of the food had been crossed off the menu board, only pie and chips or salad was left. Abigail carried her tray, containing a plate of limp-looking salad, over to a table by the window. It looks about as crisp as I feel, she thought dejectedly, looking down at the unappetising mound of food on her plate. But her morose thoughts were interrupted by Lynne, who came hurrying over.,

She perched on the edge of the table. 'Can't stop, because I'm due back,' she said in her usual rush, glancing hastily at her watch, 'but I've come over to see it.'

'See what?' asked Abigail, through a mouthful of lettuce.

'The ring, silly,' Lynne exclaimed impatiently. 'You are a dark horse, you didn't tell me you were getting married in September. And *everyone* is talking about the enormous diamonds you're wearing.'

Reluctantly Abigail put her hand on the table top, so that Lynne could inspect the ring. 'I think everyone is exaggerating,' she said, 'about the size, I mean. It's not that big.'

Lynne whistled appreciatively. 'It's a lot bigger than most girls are ever likely to get,' she said. 'It's lovely, Abigail.' Then she glanced curiously at her friend's serious expression. 'You *are* happy, aren't you?'

'Of course,' said Abigail quickly. 'I'm not feeling a hundred per cent today, that's all.' Then she changed the subject rapidly. 'How did you get on with your date with Derek Thompson?'

'Oh,' Lynne rolled her eyes heavenwards, an expression of ecastasy spread across her face, 'absolutely divine! He's a perfect honey. We're both off duty this weekend, and he's asked me down to Torquay for the whole weekend.'

Abigail raised her eyebrows. 'I always thought it was Brighton or Bournemouth that couples went for illicit weekends,' she teased.

Lynne blushed furiously. 'It's nothing like that,' she said quickly. 'We're staying with his brother, he's a consultant pathologist down there, married with two children.' She leaned across the table towards Abigail confidentially. 'That's a good sign, don't you think? Introducing me to some of his family.'

Abigail smiled at her excitement. 'I think it's a very good sign. Who knows, perhaps you'll be getting married too in the near future!'

Lynne gave an embarrassed giggle, 'I should be so lucky!' Then glancing at her watch again, she jumped down from the table. 'Must dash,' she said hastily, 'but it doesn't look as if you're going to be alone for long.'

Abigail turned her head in the direction of Lynne's

gaze. Greg Lincoln was striding through the canteen, tray in hand, obviously making for her table.

Short of picking up her tray and fleeing down the length of the canteen, there was nothing she could do but sit and wait for him to join her. However, she couldn't resist saying sarcastically. 'Do please join me,' as he sat down without asking.

'I wasn't aware that you had the monopoly of the table,' he replied, equally sarcastically.

Touchée, thought Abigail—I deserved that! However, his next words came as a surprise.

'I didn't come over to quarrel,' he said coolly, 'I came to apologise.'

'Apologise?' Startled, Abigail raised her head, grey eyes surveying this new penitent Greg rather warily.

'Yes, for provoking you last night. I shouldn't have made that jibe about your marriage.' He looked across the table, his eyes searching hers. 'Will you forgive me?'

Abigail looked down at the table top, suddenly afraid that his dark, searching gaze might see her own doubts lurking continuously at the back of her mind. 'Yes,' she muttered hesitantly, 'I suppose so.' Then she added almost inaudibly. 'I'm sorry too, for snapping back.'

'Oh, that,' he laughed. 'I deserved it.' Suddenly he reached across the table and grasped her hand. 'I don't want us to be bad friends—promise me you won't bear a grudge?'

A strange feeling of alarm made it impossible for her to look at him. The touch of his hand on hers was sending a warm glow racing through her veins, and her heart was beating ridiculously loudly against her rib cage. So loudly, it seemed to her that everyone in the canteen must surely hear it.

But to her surprise, she heard her voice replying calmly, 'I'm not the sort of person to bear grudges. It wasn't important.' She made to draw her hand away, but Greg resisted, imprisoning it with his.

'It is important to me,' he insisted, 'I want to be friends with you, *and* Rupert. Let's call a truce.'

At last Abigail looked at him. Perhaps he really was sorry for the unkind things he had said. But the enigmatic expression she encountered gave nothing away.

She smiled briefly, and said lightly, 'OK, it's a truce.'

He seemed satisfied, because he released her hand. 'Good,' he said, 'it's just as well, because I think we're going to be seeing quite a lot of each other in a little while.'

'Oh?' Abigail was puzzled. What on earth could he mean? They would see each other, of course, more or less every day in the course of their work at the hospital, but she couldn't think of any other reason.

'Rupert is overseeing some business matters for me,' he said, by way of explanation. 'It was Sir Jason that gave me the idea and . . .'

'But I don't understand what . . .' began Abigail.

'Rupert is, as I'm sure you know,' said Greg, starting on his lunch, 'quite an expert on continental property law. He'll be negotiating some contracts for Sir Jason and myself.'

'But what has that got to do with me?' queried Abigail, thoroughly mystified. 'I have nothing to do with Rupert's work.'

'Rupert has agreed to spend a month at my villa in Italy, and we have also agreed that you should be with him,' said Greg.

'He hasn't mentioned anything about it to me,' said Abigail quickly, feeling surprised that Rupert should have agreed to such a thing without mentioning it to her first. 'Anyway,' she added, 'I'm not sure whether I could get time off.'

'No problem,' said Greg confidently. 'I've already spoken to Sister Collins. You can have two weeks' holiday, and the reason Rupert hasn't told you about it yet is that we only fixed it all this morning.'

Abigail opened her mouth to protest, but he interrupted before she had a chance to speak.

'My mother and father will be there, as well as the Orchards.' He smiled at Abigail's disgruntled expression. 'Don't look so cross! Rupert thinks you could do with a good holiday, and I wholeheartedly agree. I understand you haven't had a proper one since your father died.'

Abigail clattered her knife and fork down on her plate. Between them, Rupert and Greg seemed to be organising her life, and she was not at all sure she liked it!

CHAPTER SEVEN

THE REST of the afternoon couldn't go quickly enough for Abigail. Inwardly seething, she scurried round the ward, helping settle in the new patients who arrived that afternoon. Why was Rupert making all these plans without even bothering to ask her? If this is what it's going to be like when I'm married to him, she thought rebelliously, I shall break off the engagement!

But in her heart of hearts she knew it wasn't so much the fact that he had made arrangements without conferring with her, it was because he had committed her to spending two weeks in Italy with Greg Lincoln. He was the one man she did *not* want to see too much of, they always rubbed each other up the wrong way. Any other time she would have jumped at the chance of spending a fortnight in Italy, but she would have preferred it without Greg Lincoln there, and the prospect of the presence of the Orchards didn't exactly fill her with joy!

The afternoon was busy. Dr Singh, always methodical, ordered numerous tests for the newly admitted patients, and Abigail had her work cut out to take all the bloods and get them down to the pathology laboratory in time. She knew there would be an uproar from the surgeon and the anaesthetist, if the results were not back before the scheduled oeprating time in the morning. So it with a thankful sigh that she sent the porter off to the lab with the last batch of specimens by the appointed time.

Penelope Orchard, had, as usual, been conspicuous by

her absence during all this activity. So Abigail felt no compunction about nabbing her quickly for some work the moment she clapped eyes on her.

'Hey, I need a hand with the afternoon teas,' she said.

'Oh, Abigail, you know I hate doing that,' groaned Penelope, the Cupid's bow of her lips pouting at the mere thought.

'Sorry about that, but it can't be helped,' said Abigail firmly. 'Sue Parkins is off on her study day, and there's no one else.' She started walking briskly towards the ward kitchen, a reluctant Penelope by her side. 'Come on, let's get the trolley, and please remember to put up 'nil by mouth' by the patients who are due for surgery tomorrow.'

Penelope sighed heavily. 'Honestly, Abigail, you ought to be a Sister, you're such a dragon sometimes!'

Abigail smiled sweetly, but kept her own counsel. It was not often she bullied Penelope into actually pulling her weight, but that particular afternoon she didn't see why she should work her fingers to the bone, while Penelope skived.

It was nearly time to go off duty before she had time to go back to Sister Collins' desk, to see if there was anything else that needed doing.

Sister Collins was in a surprisingly good humour. 'Mr Lincoln isn't so bad after all,' she informed an astonished Abigail. 'I find I'm getting on much better with him now. We understand each other.'

'I'm glad to hear it,' said Abigail, wondering what form of flattery Greg had been using to melt Sister Collins' heart. Then she noticed the vase of pink rosebuds on the desk, and smiled. 'They're pretty,' she said, bending to sniff their delicate fragrance.

'Mr Lincoln gave them to me,' came the reply. Sister Collins sounded pleased.

Abigail smothered a grin. So that was how Greg Lincoln had been wooing Sister Collins, and it appeared to have worked with a vengeance! Still, she reflected, it didn't matter what he did, just so long as it kept Sister happy.

'I've entered your holiday in the books,' Sister Collins continued, 'for two weeks in August. That's quite all right, I don't know why you were worried about asking me.'

'But I . . .' began Abigail in amazement, about to blurt out that it wasn't a question of being worried, but that she hadn't even known about it.

'As I told Mr Lincoln, we always close half the ward during August, and take emergency admissions only. So many of the staff take holidays at that time as it's the children's school holidays, and most patients are reluctant to come into hospital unless it's a dire emergency, for the same reason.'

'Yes, thank you,' murmured Abigail, wondering what on earth Greg had said.

'I do hope you and your fiancé have a lovely time with Mr Lincoln and his family. Of course, I shan't say a word of this to anyone else. I shall keep Mr Lincoln's confidence.'

'Thank you,' repeated Abigail, thinking the whole situation was getting more bizarre by the moment. Why should it be a confidence? Unless of course the mighty American consultant didn't want it to be known that a humble staff nurse was going along on his family holiday. Abigail wrinkled her nose at the thought. Surely Greg Lincoln wasn't a snob? But perhaps he was.

'Oh, Staff,' Sister's voice intruded in upon her confused thoughts, 'before you go off duty, could you change the sheets again for the patient in the end bed of room eighteen. It's Mr Sampson, I'm afraid he's had a little accident again. I did ask Nurse Orchard to do it, but she seems to have forgotten.'

I bet, thought Abigail cynically. Forgotten my foot! She just made sure she didn't get around to doing it. 'Has Nurse Orchard gone off duty already then?' she enquired.

'Yes,' replied Sister Collins, looking up absently from the notes she was writing. 'I said she could leave five minutes early. Sir Jason is taking his family out to the theatre in London tonight.' She gave a pleased little laugh. 'He rang me himself, and as he said, I couldn't possibly keep the great man waiting!'

But never mind about the rest of us, thought Abigail wryly, as she hurried towards the linen room. It was the third time that day she'd had the task of changing Mr Sampson's bed. The poor man was always terribly apologetic. Sister Collins had wanted to catheterise him, which would have saved a wet bed, but Greg Lincoln refused to let her. He felt it would be detrimental in the long term. In the meantime, it's definitely detrimental to *me*, thought Abigail grimly.

She had nearly reached the linen cupboard, when she literally bumped straight into Greg. 'You're in a hurry,' he remarked, as she made to move past him.

'Yes, I've got to change Mr Sampson's bed again,' said Abigail shortly, and not waiting for a reply, she opened the door of the linen cupboard and went in.

Greg followed her, watching her snatch the clean sheets and pillowcases from the shelves. 'Perhaps I'll have to catheterise him after all,' he said slowly. 'But the poor old chap's in such a state from just being in hospital that I don't want to make things worse.'

'He hasn't had major surgery,' said Abigail, turning back towards him, 'why is he in such a state?'

'Because he's worried sick that an interfering social worker won't let him go back to living alone at home,' said Greg. 'They want to put him in a home, but he wants to stay in his own house and look after his garden and his old dog.'

'I see,' said Abigail slowly. 'I didn't know that. I haven't had time to talk to him. I'm usually at the other end of the ward, and I've always been in such a rush when I've changed his bedding.'

'That's why I don't want him catheterised, because I know the social worker will take that as an indication that he's incontinent.'

'And isn't he?' asked Abigail.

'No, he isn't,' replied Greg sharply. 'He's just worried sick, out of his routine and confused. I'm determined to try to get him home as soon as possible. Back to his dog, the one living creature in the world he has to love.'

Abigail paused, the pile of linen in her arms. 'You really care, don't you?' she said quietly. She was seeing the American surgeon in a completely new light, as a truly caring and compassionate man.

'Of course I care,' answered Greg, vehemently. 'Don't you?'

'I didn't know his history,' answered Abigail truthfully, suddenly feeling ashamed that she'd always been in a hurry. So much of a hurry that she'd done whatever had been necessary for the old man, but done it automatically. 'I've been thinking of myself too much lately,' she confessed. The words were out before she could stop them, and immediately she regretted her indiscretion.

'Why?' asked Greg, homing in on to her words. 'Is

something bothering you?' He came towards her, his huge frame seeming to completely fill the small space inside the linen cupboard.

'No,' muttered Abigail hastily, 'of course there isn't.' She tried to push past him. 'Excuse me, I must go to Mr Sampson.'

'Mr Sampson won't mind waiting a few more moments,' said Greg, and without further ado he roughly took the pile of clean linen from her and plonked it on a nearby shelf. Abigail wished he wasn't so close, the distinctive smell of his aftershave was making her senses reel. 'There *is* something wrong,' he said in a low voice. 'Don't prevaricate.'

'I'm not . . . there isn't,' Abigail protested feebly, putting her slender hands up against his chest as if to ward him off as he came towards her. But it was only a token gesture. She made no real attempt to escape from his embrace. Instead, before she had realised it, she found she was automatically raising her face, her tender lips parted to receive his kiss.

As his firm mouth descended upon hers, she gave herself up to the pleasure of his kiss. It seemed he only had to touch her, to hold her, and she responded in a way she could for no other man. After a brief moment he raised his head and looked down at her, his eyes deep pools, reflecting she knew not what.

Suddenly, an image of Rupert swam muzzily before her eyes, and a red-hot feeling of guilt flooded through her. Urgently she pushed Greg aside, twisting her head away so that he couldn't see the confused anguish in her eyes.

Greg sighed, and releasing her immediately turned away. 'I'm sorry, I didn't mean to kiss you. I don't know what came over me. You're a bad influence on me,

Abigail.'

'*I'm* a bad influence on *you*?' exploded Abigail, ridiculously near to tears. 'That's ludicrous! It wasn't my fault. Why don't you just stay away from me?' She grabbed the pile of sheets and pillowcases from the shelf. 'Get out of my way,' she said woodenly.

Without another word, Greg stood aside and opened the linen cupboard door. Abigail noticed he did have the grace to look slightly uncomfortable.

'I'm sorry,' he said again as she came level with him at the doorway. 'A momentary lapse on my part—it won't happen again.'

She swept past him, then from the relative safety of the corridor she paused and said, 'I intend to speak to Rupert tonight and tell him I'm not going to Italy. Not for all the tea in China!' With that parting shot, she turned swiftly on her heels and walked quickly down the corridor towards Mr Sampson's bed.

It was true, she did intend to speak to Rupert, but of course she wouldn't be able to tell him the real reason. Just what shall I tell him? she wondered. Anyway, she reasoned sensibly, surely Greg must be having second thoughts about it now as well, because in spite of his remarks about their engagement, she knew the two men got on well together, and had a mutual respect for each other. She also knew Greg wouldn't purposely hurt Rupert.

It was just that they were so different. One rugged, dark and unpredictable, the other the perfect English gentleman. She sighed miserably, wishing Mr Wilberforce had never gone to the States, then Greg Lincoln would never have come to England on the exchange; and she would still have had her peace of mind.

Stopping by Mr Sampson's bed, she looked at the

puckered worried face of the old man. All her natural compassion rose to the surface as she remembered Greg's words, and forgetting her own problems, she spent a long time with him trying to reassure him, and generally talking, trying to draw him out of himself.

He had had a small benign tumour removed from the back of his throat, and was recovering well, but Abigail could see he was a bag of nerves.

'Don't worry about it,' she said for the umpteenth time. 'Look, I'll tell you what.' Tucking him in comfortably, she sat on the side of the bed and took the frail, blue-veined hand in hers. 'There's no need for anyone to know you've had a few little accidents, it can be our secret.'

Mr Sampson grasped her hand tightly between his gnarled fingers. 'I want to go home,' he said urgently. 'Dolly will be missing me. She's very old, you see, and nearly blind.'

'Is Dolly your dog?' asked Abigail, remembering Greg's words about him missing his dog.

'Yes,' Mr Sampson's face creased into a smile at the thought, 'Dolly is my dog. She used to be a racer, you know, best little dog on the track. Dolly Bluebird, she was called then. Of course, she's been retired for years now, and it's been just the two of us for a long time. She'll be missing me,' he repeated again sadly.

Abigail smiled gently. 'Don't worry, Mr Sampson. I know Mr Lincoln wants to get you home just as soon as possible.' She had a sudden thought, and looked in his bedside locker. There should have been a bottle in there, within easy reach for him, but it was empty.

She felt a sudden surge of anger. Trust Penelope not to bother! It was her end of the ward area, and part of her duties was to look after things like that. It suddenly became quite obvious to Abigail that, without a bottle to use, Mr Sampson had needed to press his buzzer for a nurse to come, and then hadn't been able to wait.

'I'll pop a couple of bottles into the bedside cabinet,' she said, 'then you needn't worry about calling a nurse, and you won't have any more accidents.'

'Oh, thank you, nurse!' Mr Sampson's voice was tremulous with gratitude. 'I did ask the other nurse, but she was too busy and forgot. She works very hard, you know,' he added loyally, not wanting to blame Penelope.

Abigail patted his hand, at the same time thinking, 'that's a matter of opinion!' Then she sped off down the corridor once more, loaded down with the dirty linen, collecting a couple of urine bottles on the way back and popping them in his bedside cabinet.

'There you are, nothing to worry about now,' she smiled, reassuringly at him. 'You'll be home in no time at all. You wait and see.'

Mr Sampson raised his knobbly hand in a grateful salute as Abigail left the ward and made her way back towards the changing room. Penelope is really rotten sometimes, she thought, and wondered, not for the first time, why the girl had ever bothered to go into nursing at all.

As she drove up the narrow lane, she saw Rupert's car already outside her cottage gate. Glancing at her watch, she realised she was over an hour late; he must have been waiting for ages. I'll tell him later in the evening that I'm not going to Italy, she resolved. There was no point in starting off by having an argument!

Rupert came down the path to meet her, looking concerned. 'Where have you been?' he asked. 'I've been worried.' Kissing her gently on the lips, he linked his arm through hers.

'A minor problem on the ward,' said Abigail, 'but it had to be sorted out, so I stayed.' She was tempted to say the problem had been caused by Penelope not doing her job properly, but bit her tongue, thinking that would sound too bitchy. Especially as she knew Rupert thought Penelope was a lovely girl! And who was she to disillusion him? she thought wryly.

'As long as you're safe,' said Rupert, smiling. 'I was thinking that perhaps you'd had second thoughts about me, and had skipped the country!'

Abigail looked at him sharply. That was a strange thing to say, putting into words the vague worries she had only just begun to be aware of herself. 'Don't be silly,' she said, her voice sharper than she had intended, as she unlocked the front door to let them both in.

'Only joking,' said Rupert easily.

He insisted that she sat down, and that he prepared supper for both of them, and Abigail felt too tired to protest. She was content to sit in the old, shabby armchair that had been her father's, looking out of the big bay window into the garden. But tired as she was, she couldn't still the turbulent racing of her brain.

At last she could bear it no longer. Rupert hadn't mentioned it, so she had to. 'Greg has told me you've arranged for us to go to Italy, with his family and the Orchards.'

'Yes,' answered Rupert from the kitchen, sounding very enthusiastic. 'It's a great idea, isn't it?'

'I'm not so sure,' said Abigail.

'What do you mean?' He came to the doorway, a bowl of lettuce in his hands. 'Don't you want to go? I thought it was the perfect way of combining business with pleasure.'

'I don't really want to go with Greg Lincoln, and his

family and the Orchards,' said Abigail. 'I'm not over-keen on the Orchards, and anyway, I don't think I can possibly afford it.' This last remark had come as a sudden flash of inspiration. If she said she couldn't afford it, that would be that.

'Rubbish, it's not going to cost you a penny,' said Rupert, dismissing her flimsy excuse in one breath. 'I'm getting paid, I'm taking you, and as far as not liking the Orchards, you're being ridiculous. You got on very well with them the other night. You and Penelope can go sightseeing together, when Greg, Sir Jason and I are engaged on business; it seems an ideal arrangement to me.'

Abigail sat silently mutinous in her chair, racking her brains to think of a way out, but it seemed she was to have no say in the matter at all. The very last thing she wanted was to go sightseeing with Penelope! Greg hadn't even mentioned Penelope, he had just said the Orchards. But of course, she ought to have realised, she was a fool not to have thought of it. Penelope was part of the Orchards. A whole fortnight with Penelope, that really was the last straw.

Rupert popped his head back in from the kitchen. 'Is it because you can't bear to be separated from me while I'm working?' he asked, raising his eyebrows teasingly.

Abigail tried to match his smile, not very successfully. What could she say without looking stupid and unreasonable? After all, there was no logical reason why she shouldn't want to go, she couldn't possibly tell him about Greg, and the strange effect he had on her.

'No, it's . . . oh, I don't know,' she ended up muttering lamely. Then she added, 'I suppose I'm annoyed because you arranged it all without thinking to ask me.'

Rupert laughed, and came back in from the kitchen and

knelt beside the chair, putting an arm round her shoulders. 'Darling, I do understand, and I'm sorry. But you can blame Greg for that. He's an absolute whirlwind of activity once he makes up his mind!' He picked up her hand and kissed it. 'When Greg Lincoln decides on something, he goes after it with no holds barred.'

Yes, I had noticed, reflected Abigail thoughtfully, in work *and* play! Her thoughts were interrupted by Rupert.

'I want to work on this project. It will do me a lot of good professionally. Sir Jason's is a particularly thorny problem, I'm looking forward to the challenge.' He looked at her. 'Please say you'll come. I know you'll enjoy it. We both will.'

Abigail smiled uncertainly. 'All right,' she answered reluctantly. She didn't know why, but her heart was heavy. Intuitively she felt that by saying yes, she was stepping into deep water, that they both were.

'Good girl,' said Rupert breezily. 'Come on, let's have supper, then I'll leave you in peace, as I've got some paperwork to do at home.'

As he had promised, he left almost immediately after supper, with a brief goodnight kiss. As his cool lips touched hers, Abigail momentarily wondered how it could be that the same physical act of kissing could be so different with two different men. Then guiltily she banished the errant thought from her mind, and kissed him back affectionately.

Long after Rupert had left, she sat quietly in the deep armchair by the open window. A barn owl hooted from the depths of the woodland surrounding the garden, its cry echoing eerily through the tall trees. Abigail peered out, trying to pierce the darkness, to catch a glimpse of the owl as it went about its business, the night's hunting. But it remained elusively invisible.

Her thoughts returned to Greg Lincoln. What was it Rupert had said? 'When Greg Lincoln decides on something, he goes after it with no holds barred.'—yes, that was it. The main problem was, did she know for certain what it was that Greg had decided?

The barn owl hooted again, the sound floating into the house from the still blackness of the night. Suddenly Abigail was filled with the image of the fieldmice, hiding out there in the long grass, frightened to move because of the sound of the owl. How awful it must be to be hunted, not to know which way to turn for safety. Suddenly Greg's face flashed before her mind's eye. 'No holds barred,' Rupert had said, ruthless like the barn owl!

With a sudden irritable movement she stood up, closed the window, and swished the curtains across, shutting out the night. Don't be ridiculous, she told herself firmly, you're no mouse, and Greg Lincoln isn't a bird of prey! Although the somewhat sinister simile remained disturbingly with her, as she made her way upstairs to bed.

CHAPTER EIGHT

THE THREE weeks before the Italian trip disappeared quickly; Rupert flying out earlier with Sir Jason and Lady Orchard, and of course Penelope. Although how Penelope had managed to wangle the extra time off, a whole month in the middle of the busiest period, Abigail didn't know. She supposed Sir Jason and Greg had put pressure on the Senior Nursing Officer. What it is to have friends and relations in high places! she reflected drily.

'I'll take good care of Rupert for you,' Penelope had told Abigail blithely, the day before their departure.

'Thanks,' Abigail had replied shortly, Penelope's smug, supercilious smile doing nothing to improve her ill humour.

It was leading up to the time of the bed closures for August, which meant all the surgeons were squashing in semi-urgent cases, trying to rush through the patients needing minor surgery before the beginning of August. This meant a very rapid turnover in the bed state, and a heavy workload for everyone, most of all for the nurses on the wards.

'Half of these patients could be done in the day surgical unit,' grumbled Sister Collins one morning, as she and Abigail were updating the Kardex system yet again. 'I keep telling the consultants that they should have pressed for another operating session in the day unit—the one the GU surgeons have just managed to acquire.'

'Yes,' agreed Abigail, 'but I understand they do have

a tremendously long waiting list. Their wards are always more crowded than ours.'

'If they were a little better organised, they could turn over their patients as fast as we do,' replied Sister Collins severely.

Abigail smiled wryly; their own good organisation was due in no small measure to Greg, rather than Sister Collins. 'Never mind, it's a good job some of us are well organised,' she said, flipping the last Kardex card into place. 'It would do them good, Sister Collins, to have you around on the GU ward for a month, you'd soon get those housemen on their toes!'

Sister Collins looked up sharply. 'I sincerely hope you're not serious,' she muttered. 'A month on that ward would give me a nervous breakdown!'

Abigail laughed. 'I was only joking,' she said, 'although seriously, they do need someone like you or Mr Lincoln. If he was their consultant, the housemen wouldn't forget to do chest X-rays, or send the bloods down to the pathology lab on time.'

'Mr Lincoln certainly wouldn't tolerate the slipshod habits of the GU housemen,' agreed Sister Collins. Then her face broke into one of her rare smiles. 'And somehow I think it would be the housemen who had the nervous breakdowns, not our Mr Lincoln!'

Abigail agreed, noting the way Sister Collins had said 'our Mr Lincoln' in quite a proprietorial and proud way. It was obvious that she had eventually taken him to her heart; and on reflection she supposed this was not altogether surprising. Greg Lincoln could be devastatingly charming when he so chose.

'Have you got everything fixed up for your holiday?' enquired Sister.

'Yes,' Abigail replied briefly. It was the first time Sister had mentioned it since the day she had told her that the leave had been granted. And Abigail hadn't discussed the forthcoming holiday with anyone, not even her closest friend Lynne.

Not that Lynne would have been all that interested—she'd hardly seen anything of her, as she was now totally absorbed in her new romance with Derek Thompson. It seemed to have blossomed into something serious with a vengeance. Whenever Abigail had bumped into her in the canteen, she had always been with Derek, and Abigail had usually made an excuse to go and sit with other friends, leaving the two of them alone. It was quite obvious to everyone that the old saying 'two's company, three's a crowd' applied in their case.

As she watched them leave the canteen one day, little fingers linked in a private intimate way, a chilly feeling of inexplicable sadness swept over Abigail. It was lovely to see them so very much in love, and it made her wish it could be like that for her and Rupert. She was happy with Rupert, very happy, but not ecstatic; not the way Lynne and Derek were.

I'll feel much happier when I get to Italy and see Rupert again, she told herself firmly, as the canteen doors swung shut, blotting out the sight of Lynne and Derek.

She had only spoken to him once, very briefly on the telephone, since he had been in Italy, but he had seemed to be enjoying himself. That night Abigail rang him again. He sounded so loving, and was so sensible and reasonable, that she started feeling better, and in spite of everything even began to look forward a little to the trip. Rupert had told her that the airline tickets would be sent to her, and she would be met at the Linate airport in Milan.

After she had put the phone down that night, Abigail smiled at her reflection in the mirror hanging above the telephone. She had been foolish in her imaginings of impending doom, nothing would go wrong—how could it? And as for Greg—well, she hadn't seen much of him recently either, as they'd been so busy that he'd been tied up in the operating theatre for long periods at a stretch, and she'd been working on the ward at a permanent gallop!

Abigail assumed that he would be going on ahead of her, to join his father and mother, and that she would be the last one to join the party at the villa. However, with just one day to go before she was sheduled to fly out, she still hadn't received the airline tickets, and Greg was still working in the hospital.

There was nothing for it but to ask him if he knew what was happening, so rather reluctantly, she stopped him after the morning ward round. She was very conscious of the curious eyes of the junior medical staff, all focused with unblinking gaze on them, eager as always to pick up the latest piece of gossip. So she said very formally, 'May I have a word with you, Mr Lincoln?'

'Certainly,' he replied equally formally, gesturing to the juniors that they could leave. 'Come into my office.'

One of the junior doctors, a girl, giggled, and Abigail glowered at her. She was well aware the three-quarters of the females in the hospital thought Greg Lincoln was the dishiest thing on two legs, and that probably the junior doctors in question thought that she, Abigail, was of the same opinion! Well, she was *not*, and flashing the errant giggler another withering glance, she followed Greg into his office.

'Rupert told me that the airline ticket would be sent to me,' she said hesitantly, 'but I haven't received it yet, and I was wondering if you . . .'

'I thought you didn't want to go,' he replied with an irritating grin.

'I . . . well, I *am* going, as you very well know,' said Abigail, exasperated by his grin, partly because she knew she was grinning back. 'That is,' she added, 'if I ever get the ticket.'

'I've got it,' said Greg casually, tapping the briefcase on his desk. 'We'll be going together.'

'Together?' Her surprised voice echoed round the office.

'Do you mind?'

'I . . . er . . . no, of course not. But I thought you . . .' she paused, collecting her thoughts, the wind being momentarily taken out of her sails. 'I thought you would be travelling earlier to be with your parents,' she said at last.

'No,' he answered, pulling a pile of papers towards him. 'Now, is there anything else? I've got a lot to do before we go.' The tone of his voice was almost curt, not quite, but most certainly dismissive.

'No,' said Abigail, turning to go. But Greg's voice called her back.

'Oh, by the way, I forgot to tell you. It's not going to be all play, you know.'

Abigail turned round to face him. 'I know,' she began, 'you and Rupert have business to attend to.'

'I shall be doing laser surgery in Siena,' he said, sorting through his papers, 'and as you will be there, I thought you could be my theatre nurse. I prefer to use an English-trained girl.'

There was silence, and he raised his head to look at her. 'You've had theatre training, haven't you?' he asked abruptly.

'Well, yes, but . . .' Abigail suddenly felt panic-stricken.

She never knew what surprise Greg was going to spring on her next. 'I've never even seen laser surgery,' she said. 'I don't think I . . .'

'Don't worry about that. You're not going to do the surgery,' he replied, raising his eyebrows wryly. 'All you have to do is be there, and hand me whatever I ask for. Your part of the procedure will be exactly the same as for any other orthodox operation.' He looked at her quizzically. 'Don't tell me you're not capable of that!'

'Of course I'm capable,' Abigail flashed back proudly, 'it's just that I'm surprised. Is there anything else you haven't told me?'

'Not that I can think of,' came the absentminded reply, he was sorting once more through the papers, 'but I'll let you know if I think of anything.'

'Thank you,' said Abigail, leaving the office quickly. What a cheek that damned man had, springing that on her! I'd better brush up my theatre technique with a textbook, she thought, realising she'd have to take the wretched thing on holiday with her. She hurried down the corridor. The last thing she wished to do was make a fool of herself in front of Greg, and an operating theatre full of Italians.

Later in the day she was at the nursing station filing the latest batch of pathology reports, when Greg walked by. 'Be ready at seven o'clock in the morning,' he said, not stopping. 'And be prompt. I'll organise everything else.'

'So nice of you,' said Abigail, her voice edged with sarcasm. 'I don't know what I'd do without you!'

He threw back his dark head and roared with laughter, causing several patients to look over with curiosity. 'Stop looking so bad-tempered,' was his only reply as he strode on down towards the end rooms of the ward.

Abigail scowled in a most unladylike fashion at his retreating back, then bent over her paperwork. He'd had the last word as usual! However, she was very careful to make sure she was ready at the appointed time, which was just as well, as Greg was punctual to the very minute.

As they drove to Heathrow, Greg told her they would pick up a hired car at Milan, then drive down the autostrada to the villa, which was situated on the shore of Lago di Trasimeno. Abigail's feelings were a mixture of apprehension and excitement as the journey to Italy began. There would be so much to see, and of course she would be with Rupert again. She hoped they would have plenty of time for sightseeing together, just the two of them.

The arrangements Greg had made unfolded with clockwork precision, and soon they had left Milan airport far behind and were speeding down the autostrada in brilliant sunshine.

'Looking forward to seeing Rupert?' asked Greg suddenly, keeping his eyes on the road ahead.

'Yes, of course,' said Abigail truthfully. 'I'm hoping that he and I will be able to do some exploring, I'd like to see as much as possible.'

'You will,' replied Greg. 'I've got quite a few trips lined up for us, plus of course the visit to the hospital in Siena, which will be just you and I.'

Abigail remained silent. What exactly did Greg mean by 'us'? she wondered. She hoped he didn't mean that she and Rupert would have to spend all their time with Greg and Penelope. Suddenly, the sinking feeling she'd had before returned to the pit of her stomach. She had a horrible feeling everything was going to be organised for her, and that she wouldn't have a say in anything.

However, she didn't voice her doubts, merely remarking,

'won't it be a little difficult explaining laser surgery?—the language barrier, I mean,' she added by way of explanation.

'I speak pretty good Italian,' answered Greg. 'My mother is Italian, remember?'

'I didn't know you could speak the language—you never said.'

'There's a great deal you don't know about me,' came the reply.

That's true, reflected Abigail, as she sat back and watched the flat plain of Lombardy, the rice-fields separated by the straight lines of poplars flashing past. Soon the lush flat fields gave way to the rolling patchwork hills around Florence, and they were negotiating the bends on the impressive viaducts which linked the peaks of the Appenines. Abigail gave up worrying about the two weeks ahead, and began to enjoy the scenery. From Florence they descended once more into a valley, the fields crammed with orderly rows of sunflowers, their serried ranks turned with one accord towards the heat of the sun, the brilliant yellow of their faces enhanced by the purple blue background of the distant mountains.

As they drew near their destination she began to wonder if Rupert would be there to meet her, and also what would Greg's mother and father be like. She hoped they wouldn't be as stuffy as Sir Jason and Lady Orchard! And of course, Penelope would be there, no doubt looking elegantly suntanned, thought Abigail, looking down at her own pale-skinned arms. She also idly wondered what sort of villa it could be. Fairly large, she assumed, because of the host of people that would be staying together under one roof.

But in spite of all her imagining and wonderings, she

was totally unprepared for the beauty of the scene that met her eyes, as Greg's car drove into the courtyard of an enormous villa and pulled to a halt on shiny cobbles. The villa was located just outside the fortress walls of the small lakeside town called Castiglione del Lago, which clung, with the tenacity born of ages, to the craggy rocks overlooking the lake.

Rupert came running out into the courtyard. 'I heard the car,' he said, hugging and kissing Abigail. He took her arm. 'Come and look at the view, it's quite fantastic.'

Abigail walked with him across to the grey stone wall, chipped and flaking with age, which surrounded the courtyard, her arm comfortably tucked through his. She felt secure again, now that she was with Rupert; she was happy. He loved her, and that was enough. Together they leaned on the wall, looking at the vista of the smooth waters of the lake, reflecting the brilliant blue of the sky. The mirror-smooth blue stretched as far as the eye could see, its surface broken only by the white sails of the small sailing dinghies, fluttering about like a host of moths, as they tried to catch the slightest breeze. It was very hot, the only sound from their perch high above the lake was the whirring of cicadas, filling the air; the noise seeming to come from all sides. Abigail craned her head, looking up into the thick branches of the umbrella pines shading the courtyard, but the cicadas remained elusive.

As Greg came over and joined them, he noticed Abigail looking upwards. 'It's a rare thing to see one,' he remarked, referring to the cicadas, 'and even if you do it's a disappointment. They make an exciting sound, but they're very ordinary to look at.'

Abigail glanced at him. His bare arm was resting against hers, and instinctively she edged a little closer to Rupert;

at the same time thinking how well Greg blended in with the brilliant colours of the Italian landscape. With his tanned skin, and jet black hair, he looked completely at home. But then, she reminded herself, he was at home in a way, because he was half Italian.

She turned to Rupert. 'Where is Penelope?' she asked. 'Is she out with her parents?'

For a brief moment he looked strangely elusive, then he laughed. 'She's resting. I'm afraid we had rather a late night last night.'

'Oh?' Abigail deliberately put the question mark in the exclamation. She wasn't used to Rupert looking that way, if it had been anyone else she would have called it distinctly shifty.

He laughed again, faintly uneasily, or so it seemed to her ears. 'You've no idea how persuasive Penelope can be. She insisted we drove for miles to some restaurant she knew!'

'I have a very good idea—you forget I work with her,' observed Abigail drily.

While she had been awaiting the arrival of Greg, Penelope had obviously been making full use of Rupert's company. He would be no match for Penelope's wiles if she put her mind to it. But relationships must be based on trust, she reminded herself, and she trusted Rupert, so she gave him an affectionate smile and squeezed his arm.

'Let's get my luggage,' she said, starting back towards the car.

Greg was already there, heaving the mounds of luggage out of the small boot. I hope Penelope transfers her attention to you, thought Abigail, watching his tall muscular frame as he held a suitcase with ease under each arm. Although even as the thought passed through her head, she knew that Greg was not the type of man to be manipulated by anyone, man or woman! Rather the reverse; he always seemed to be doing the manipulating.

'Come on,' said Greg over his shoulder. 'Rupert, you can bring the rest. Just time to get unpacked before lunch.' This last remark was addressed to Abigail.

She followed Greg's tall figure into the cool interior of the villa. Inside everything was light and airy; the walls were whitewashed and the floors covered in red polished tiles. Large terracotta urns with trailing green ferns spilling out of them were the only decoration, apart from the occasional tapestry hung on the stark whiteness of the walls. It was utter simplicity, and yet gave a feeling of opulence. As she followed his figure up a winding staircase, Abigail wondered whether Greg had decided on the decor, or whether he had hired someone to do it for him.

Almost as if he had read her thoughts, he said, 'Do you like it? I decorated it myself.'

'It's lovely,' said Abigail, smiling, 'absolutely perfect.'

'High praise indeed,' replied Greg, raising one dark eyebrow. 'At last I've done something that pleases you! Lunch is at one o'clock sharp,' he added, dumping her bags in the middle of the bedroom, 'down on the patio.'

The vine-covered patio, where the assembled company sat down to lunch, was on the other side of the house, and had a differently angled view of the magnificent lake. Abigail wondered how many maids there were, as two different girls served them with lunch, which was an enormous affair, washed down with plenty of wine and mineral water.

The Orchards sat at the far end of the table, and after briefly acknowledging Abigail largely ignored her presence. Penelope waved gaily, then also appeared to forget she existed. But Abigail liked Greg's mother. She was a vivacious, friendly woman, obviously in her element with a large family at the meal table.

'She's more Italian than the Italians who live here,' grumbled Greg's father affectionately, looking at his wife.

'That's because she spends most of the time in America,' said Greg with a grin.

'Now that you've bought the land as well as the villa,' replied his father, 'I can see I shall be forced to spend much more of my time here.'

'Come on,' said Greg, teasing his father, 'don't pretend you don't like it. I know you love Italy just as much, if not more, than Mother.'

Abigail looked at Greg; his father's words had slowly sunk in. 'Bought the land?' she queried. 'But I thought that was why Rupert came out here.'

'Oh, he did,' said Greg blandly, 'but it came on to the market a little sooner than expected. However, I shall still need some help with tying up the legal side.'

Abigail looked at him suspiciously. She had her doubts. Did he really need Rupert to help with the legal side of things? Personally, she thought Greg seemed more than capable of sorting out anything for himself.

'As we shall conclude the business side of things much sooner than expected,' he continued smoothly, ignoring her questioning gaze, 'we shall all be free to enjoy our holiday. I understand Rupert has already completed Sir Jason's transactions satisfactorily.'

Abigail glanced at Rupert, seated at the far end of the table; but he was deeply involved in an animated conversation with Penelope and her father, and for all the notice he had taken of Abigail during the meal, she might just as well have not been there. It's not his fault, though, thought Abigail loyally. Greg's mother had arranged the seating, and Rupert had been placed away from her with the Orchards.

She looked back at Greg, to find his dark eyes surveying her with an implacable expression. She was certain he knew what she was thinking, that Rupert was payng more attention to Penelope than he was to her, his fiancée.

'Rupert has become very friendly with the Orchards,' he observed to her chagrin, adding in a low voice meant for her ears only, 'You don't mind, do you?'

She felt her cheeks colouring, and was angry with herself for giving her feelings away so easily. 'Of course not,' she answered primly. 'Why should I?'

Greg's mouth twisted into a grin. 'Naturally, I assumed you would be interested in Rupert's affairs,' he said casually.

'Of course I am,' replied Abigail, equally casually, even though her nerves felt raw-edged at his deliberate play on words. 'But there are affairs, and affairs!' Fixing a noncommittal blank expression on her face, she sipped her wine, although how she forced herself to swallow it she didn't know. There was an uncomfortable lump at the back of her throat, which was threatening to choke her.

She was thankful when the meal had finished and she could get away from Greg's subtle needling. Everyone retired to their rooms for a siesta. It was even hotter by now, and Abigail stripped down to her brief underwear and flung herself on the bed. The windows of her balcony were wide open, and a faint refreshing breeze blew in from the lake. It seemed a long time ago that Greg had picked her up at the cottage that morning, and as for the ENT ward—well, that might as well be in another lifetime. She smiled sleepily, wondering what Sue Parkins would say if she knew Staff Nurse Pointer was in Italy with the

Orchards and their new consultant, Mr Lincoln! Then the effects of the food and the strong red wine, plus the constant whirring of cicadas, took their toll, lulling her to sleep along with the rest of the household.

A discreet tap on her door awakened her. 'Abigail.' It was Greg's voice, 'Abigail, are you awake?'

Hastily Abigail struggled to a sitting position; how long had she been asleep? The sun was still shining brilliantly across the faintly rippling waters of the lake, and the ever-present cicadas were still chirruping as busily as ever.

Greg repeated her name. 'Abigail?'

'Yes, just a moment.' Hastily she snatched at her cotton house-robe which was lying across the top of the bed, and flung it on. Then padding across to the door in her bare feet, she cautiously opened it a crack and peered out. 'What do you want?'

He laughed. 'Aren't you going to invite me in?' Slipping his hand through the open crack, he teasingly ruffled her hair, still tousled from sleep. 'You look half asleep.'

'I would still have been asleep if you hadn't woken me,' she confessed awkwardly, feeling unsure of his teasing, and distinctly at a disadvantage in her half-dressed state. It had been one thing dealing with Greg in the familiar environment of the hospital, but now in this place, in his villa, she was on strange unfamiliar ground.

'Well, can I come in?' he asked again, 'or are you afraid of being alone with me?'

'Of course not,' she countered defensively, swinging the bedroom door wide open just to show him she meant what she said.

'Oh, I was thinking that perhaps you might be.' His voice was teasing, and his eyes sparkling with wicked humour at her expense.

Abigail pulled the flimsy cotton robe tightly around her and tied the belt securely. Trying to appear unselfconscious, although her legs felt about as mobile as wooden stilts, she walked across to the balcony, and leaning on the balustrade, pretended to look at the view across the lake. In reality, however, the panorama swam in a misty haze, as all she could think of was that Greg was much too close.

He had joined her on the balcony, his arm lazily encircling her waist; she tried not to breathe in the heady smell of his skin with its distinctive musky perfume of aftershave.

'Where's Rupert?' she asked, adroitly side-stepping out of reach of his encircling arm.

She wasn't looking at him, but she heard his breath expelled in a long-drawn-out sigh as he replied, 'Ah yes—Rupert.'

The sound of his footsteps retreated back across the floor of her room towards the door, and she turned; unaware of the lovely picture she made, framed on the balcony against the sunlit blue of the lake.

'I came to tell you we're going out,' he said quietly. 'Penelope is impatient to go, and she and Rupert are waiting in the courtyard. Do you want to come, or shall I tell them to go on?'

'Oh no, of course I want to come,' said Abigail quickly. 'Tell them I'll be five minutes.' She ran quickly across the room to close the door behind him. 'I won't keep them waiting,' she promised.

'I'll tell them,' said Greg, disappearing along the corridor that led to the stairs.

Quickly splashing cold water on her face to freshen herself, Abigail took the coolest dress she could find from her wardrobe—a dark blue cheesecloth dress, loosely tied at the waist with a rope belt. She literally flung it on, then dragged a brush through her hair, not even bothering to stop and look in the mirror, just remembering to grab a pair of sunglasses as she was leaving the room.

She flew headlong down the stairs and arrived breathless in the sun-filled courtyard, only to find it empty. No sign of anyone, and only one car, Greg's, standing in the shade cast by the pines. Abigail skidded to an abrupt halt, looking around the deserted courtyard in puzzlement. Surely they couldn't have got tired of waiting? She had said five minutes, and in fact was sure she'd been even less.

Slowly she paced the uneven cobbles towards the shade by the wall, trying to contain her bitter disappointment that they hadn't waited. Then suddenly she saw Greg, standing at the far end of the wall, in a dense patch of shade. He turned at the sound of her soft footsteps on the cobbles.

'Penelope wanted to go shopping in Perugia,' he said, indicating the empty courtyard. 'I couldn't face it, so Rupert very kindly offered to take her.'

'But what about me?' demanded Abigail, suddenly feeling angry. 'I might have wanted to go shopping, did you think of that?'

'Rupert said you *hated* shopping,' he replied, raising his eyebrows at her indignation. 'I thought as your fiancé, he ought to have an accurate idea of what you did or didn't like.'

Abigail pursed her lips, unable to reply to the overt dig, knowing it was probably true that Rupert had said that. After all, she was always telling him she hated shopping. 'What's so special about the shops in Perugia?' she asked at last, biting back the temptation to snap his head off with great difficulty.

'Nothing,' said Greg, smiling as he came to join her. 'There's a large department store, not large by our standards, just by local standards. Apparently there's nothing Penelope likes better than to meander around foreign shops.' Courteously he opened the car door for her to get in. 'I've arranged to meet them in Assisi tonight for a drink, I thought you'd prefer the sights of Assisi to a shopping expedition; I'm sorry I was wrong.'

Abigail felt foolish, it was all so reasonable, and of course she would much prefer to see Assisi rather than look at shops. What was she making a fuss about?

'Do Rupert and Penelope know where to meet us?' she asked.

'Of course,' replied Greg. 'Penelope and Rupert know the bar well. It was Penelope's choice, as a matter of fact. She's been often with Rupert.'

Abigail glanced at him quickly, as he motioned her into the car. She knew, of course, that Penelope and Rupert had been thrown together, but the way Greg had said 'often' caused a jagged barb of doubt to strike suddenly at her heart. She had never seriously doubted Rupert before, indeed she'd never had any cause to. He had always been so reliable; it was always Rupert who had been the strong one, comforting her whenever doubts had assailed her. But now, suddenly, he no longer seemed the firm anchor of strength she had come to rely on. Although she told herself she was being quite ridiculous to read so much into one little word.

Greg swung the car round the courtyard, its tyres shrieking in protesting squeals on the shiny cobbles, and then they were off, down the steep hillside leading from the villa to the road running along the side of the lake. Abigail's thoughts were chaotic, all her long-submerged worries suddenly surfaced; her own attitude to Greg, who managed to infuriate her most of the time, and yet at the same time remain so maddeningly attractive. And now the worry that Rupert might have become infatuated with Penelope. She sighed, not knowing what to make of it, and suddenly wished she was back in the familiar routine of the ENT ward, rescuing Sue Parkins from some disaster. At least there everything was clearcut, the course of action needed was always obvious . . but here, that was another matter!

Greg looked across at her. 'Why the sigh, Abigail?' he asked. 'Don't you like Italy?'

'I like it very much, at least what I've seen of it so far,' answered Abigail, glad to be able to speak the truth about something. But she couldn't possibly tell him why she had sighed, couldn't tell him what a muddle her thoughts were in, because he was inextricably mixed up in it all. Although thank goodness he didn't have an inkling of the effect he had on her, even if he did have his own suspicions about Rupert and Penelope.

'It's nothing,' she muttered at last, and turned to look out of the window.

'Why don't you just sit back and relax and enjoy the holiday? Take advantage of whatever comes your way, and leave it at that,' he suggested. 'You're much too intense, you know, much too serious.'

'I can't help the way I am,' said Abigail, knowing that he spoke sense, but not wanting to listen. 'It's my nature, I can't change.'

'You could always try,' he said with a smile. 'Come on, Abigail, the ENT ward is far behind you. Enjoy yourself, instead of looking as if you're personally shouldering all the troubles of the world!'

Suddenly he pulled the car to a halt at the side of the road, beneath the overhanging boughs of a huge white oleander. The branches quivered, cascading the fragrant petals like confetti down on to the windscreen. Reaching across, he caught her chin between his thumb and forefinger.

'Smile,' he commanded decisively.

His dark eyes had laughing glints in their depths, as he gazed down into her troubled grey ones, and against her will Abigail found herself smiling back. 'That's better,' was his verdict. Then he gently brushed her lips with his, in a strangely passionless way. 'Now stop worrying. Surely you can be happy here, in this lovely place.' He ran a finger down her cheek.

Abigail felt strangely comforted by his gentle gesture. 'Yes, I should be,' she admitted, 'but Rupert and I . . .'

'I'm not going to pry into your affairs,' Greg said quietly, but very firmly. He started up the car engine again. 'You and Rupert have your own lives to lead, only you two can do that.'

After that, the tension between them eased, and Greg proved to be an interesting and knowledgeable companion; pointing out the many places of interest as they drove along. Finally he pointed to the outline of Assisi itself, sprawled on the slopes of Mount Subasio, basking in the clear sunlight of Umbria.

As they drew nearer, Abigail exclaimed in delight. The shape became clearly defined into a mass of houses, towers, streets and belfries, the great Basilica of St Francis dominating everything. The rocks and stones of the building were a delicate warm, pinky grey, the colour of the ancient crustaceans that once lived there, millions of years before.

Greg smiled at Abigail's cries of delight. 'Better than shopping?' he asked softly.

'Much better,' Abigail agreed happily.

CHAPTER NINE

THE TREASURES inside the Basilica of St Francis were absorbing, and by the time Abigail allowed herself to be persuaded to leave, albeit reluctantly, the warm pink dusk of evening had suffused the hilltop town, the buildings glowing in the last remaining rays of the dying sun.

'Oh, goodness,' Abigail exclaimed guiltily, 'I didn't realise I'd taken so long!'

Greg smiled. 'It seemed a pity to dampen your enthusiasm,' he said, 'but don't worry, we're not late. I daresay Rupert and Penelope are a drink ahead of us. I can't see Penelope waiting.'

It seemed a crime to hurry. So they dawdled in the velvety evening air, meandering through the cobbled streets. The house-martins and swallows dived and screamed overhead, snatching at small insects rash enough to fly before the shafts of sunlight. The wrought iron street lamps cast their yellow glow on the uneven cobbles, and beneath every lamp sat a group of women knitting; always surrounded by a crowd of noisy children and a motley assortment of dogs.

'This is an enchanted place,' whispered Abigail, almost afraid to speak too loudly in case she broke the spell.

'You think so?' said Greg. Then he smiled gently, and taking her hand in his held it loosely. 'I think Italy has already begun to weave its magic spell over you,' he observed. 'Already you seem much more relaxed.'

Abigail laughed, her grey eyes sparkling. She didn't

remove her hand, it felt comfortable in his, and for the moment she felt ridiculously happy. But it was only a moment, a few seconds later that moment was shattered as Greg pointed towards a little bar in the main piazza.

'There, what did I tell you? They *are* one drink ahead of us.' Abigail looked in the direction of his pointing finger. Then she saw them, sitting very close together, a single candle in a glass holder illuminating their faces, which even though she was some distance away, she could see were animated and very intimate. She hung back, not wanting to break into the circle of intimacy that surrounded them; but Greg continued to walk and there was no alternative but to accompany him.

As they drew nearer, she could hear their low voices laughing and talking, and it was only a long time afterwards, almost towards the end of the evening, that she realised Greg had discreetly let go of her hand the moment they had seen Rupert and Penelope. Not that she had attached any importance to that, there was nothing romantic about the way he had held her hand, it was just a friendly gesture, like that of a brother. And anyway, at the time she had only been conscious of the rapt expression on Rupert's face as he listened to his companion.

It was Penelope who saw them first. She waved gaily, and broke into her tinkly laugh, breaking the peaceful serenity of the piazza. At least, so it seemed to Abigail's sensitive ears.

'We've had an absolutely fantastic time,' she said, as Greg pulled out a chair for Abigail and they joined the two of them at the table. 'Have you?'

'Yes,' Greg answered for them both, then turned to Rupert. 'Hope you didn't suffer too much. Being dragged around shops by a woman is my idea of hell on earth!'

'He *loved* it,' said Penelope firmly, laying a well manicured hand possessively on Rupert's arm. 'And I dare you to say you didn't.'

'I did love every minute of it,' replied Rupert, grinning, then suddenly, as if he'd just remembered Abigail's presence, he smiled at her too, adding hastily, 'I thought you'd enjoy sightseeing better. I hope you didn't mind.'

'As it happens you were right, but I would have preferred to have been asked!' Abigail replied, a touch of acerbity tinged her voice, and she noticed a guilty expression flicker across Rupert's face.

'Shall we order a drink?' interrupted Greg, as Rupert opened his mouth to reply. Not waiting for an answer from the others, he called a waiter over to their table. 'Campari and soda for me,' he said. 'What about you, Abigail?'

'I'll have the same,' she answered, noticing how grateful Rupert looked for the interruption. She wondered whether Greg had done it on purpose, or whether it was just fortuitous that he happened to speak at that moment.

'I'll have a small beer,' said Rupert quickly, keeping his gaze averted from Abigail's clear grey eyes.

'And I'll have an *enormous* gin and a little tonic,' said Penelope. She slid her arm around Greg's neck, and kissed him on the cheek. 'You will buy me an enormous gin, won't you?' she purred provocatively.

'I'll buy you anything you want,' said Greg with a laugh, appearing to enjoy her attention, 'and I'm sure that goes for Rupert too.'

Penelope giggled delightedly. 'I'm lucky to have two such attentive men, but I mustn't be selfish. You must spoil Abigail too.'

Oh, heavens, thought Abigail with a sinking feeling, this

is going to be an awful evening. She hated girls who deliberately turned on the 'little girl' charm and flirted with men, it was something she could never do.

'I don't feel the need to be spoiled,' she said coldly. 'You're welcome to them both, Penelope, if that's what you want.' It was a bitchy remark, and out of character, but at that particular moment she could have quite cheerfully spat blood!

The awkward silence at the table was broken by Greg giving the order to the waiter, who had been hovering attentively near by. Abigail bent her head to hide her furious expression, and fondled the ears of a black and white dog who was sitting, looking expectant, by their table.

'I wouldn't touch the dogs around here,' said Penelope in her supercilious tone, the one she reserved for elderly patients and foreigners. 'For a start they're not well bred, and you never know what you might catch.'

'Penelope's right,' chimed in Rupert. 'You never know . . .'

'No, you don't, do you?' said Abigail quietly.

Rupert flushed uneasily, and she knew the innuendo had gone home. 'I worry about you,' he said defensively. 'You don't want to be ill while you're away.'

'I daresay the dogs here are as healthy as anywhere,' said Greg, and picking up a pretzel from the dish on the table, he tossed it to the dog, who snapped it up eagerly.

He had broken a potentially awkward situation again, and this time Abigail knew he had done so on purpose, and was grateful. She was feeling confused and angry, and the last thing she wanted to do was quarrel with Rupert. When we're on our own, we'll be able to talk reasonably, and sensibly, and everything will be all right, she told herself; controlling the upsurge of jealousy that threatened to swamp her, with an effort.

So she smiled at Rupert, and was glad to see him smile back, relief written all over his face. He had never been faced with an acid-tongued Abigail before, and she couldn't help thinking, just a little bit smugly, that he didn't know how to handle her in that mood! Almost simultaneously, though, the uncomfortable thought flashed across her mind that Greg would have known exactly how to handle it—he would have lashed back and they would have had a flaming row! In a strangely contradictory way, she wished she and Rupert had rowed there and then, and to hell with the embarrassment!

But for the rest of the hour they spent at the bar, Abigail made a point of being sweetness and light itself; so much so that Greg leaned over at one point and whispered in her ear, 'Be careful, or you'll go over the top!''

Abigail rewarded him with a shrivelling glance as Penelope asked, 'What did you say, Greg?'

'Give the dog another biscuit,' he replied, with a deadpan face.

Abigail couldn't help it, she giggled. He looked so serious, and picking up a handful of pretzels, she started feeding them to the dog one by one.

'Pongo!' shouted the waiteer, and the dog pricked up its ears, then slunk sheepishly away along the edge of the square.

'Tell him it's my fault,' pleaded Abigail, clutching hold of Greg's arm anxiously. 'He didn't beg for food, I offered it.'

Greg laughed, and said something in rapid Italian to the waiter, who beamed from ear to ear and whistled the dog back, giving it a friendly cuff around the ears as it came bounding back up to the table. As he made out their bill, he continued chatting to Greg.

'What did he say?' asked Abigail when he'd gone.

'He said the dog always picks on the pretty English girls, because he knows they're soft-hearted,' answered Greg, smiling widely.

'*I'm* not soft-hearted,' said Penelope.

You can say that again, thought Abigail, biting back the words with difficulty. It seemed that neither Greg nor Rupert heard Penelope's remark, as they made no comment.

Rupert merely remarked mildly to Abigail. 'You'll be partly to blame for that animal's premature middle-aged spread!'

Abigail laughed and linked her arm through his. 'Dogs don't worry about their figures,' she said.

Rupert smiled down at her, and she felt some of her old happiness return. She had an over-active imagination, that was her problem, she decided. But when they reached the parked car, she wasn't certain whether or not it was her imagination that Rupert hesitated just a second before opening the door of his car for her. For a moment she had almost thought he was going to usher Penelope into the car, but then, as she told herself later, it was a natural mistake. He had arrived with Penelope, and she with Greg, but she drove back to the villa with Rupert. On the way he seemed to be his old self, explaining what he had been doing while waiting for her to arrive, and Abigail's worries evaporated—she definitely had an over-active imagination, something she would have to curb in the future.

The days passed quickly one after the other, there was so much to do, sailing, windsurfing, sightseeing, and always they ended the day sitting late into the evening on the patio, eating and drinking under a star-spangled sky.

Abigail was pleased that Rupert had finished his work for Sir Jason, and so had plenty of time to spend relaxing, although she did sometimes wish they could have more time together, just the two of them. She had hoped, after the departure of Sir Jason and Lady Orchard, that Penelope would spend more time with Greg, but it seemed that everything had always been arranged, and it was always a foursome. Rupert didn't appear to mind at all, and on the few occasions Abigail had mentioned it to him, he had said they couldn't very well be rude as they were staying in Greg's villa.

One particular morning, however, when Abigail went down to breakfast, she found herself alone on the patio. From the debris of crumbs and half-empty glasses of orange littering the table, it was obvious that everyone else had already breakfasted.

Pouring herself a glass of fresh orange juice, she wandered slowly to the edge of the patio, leaning on the balustrade overlooking the lake. Suddenly, a movement far down below caught her eye; it was Penelope and Rupert running down the slope towards the boathouse on the shore of the lake. They had their arms linked, and their laughter floated up clearly through the still morning air. Abigail bit her lip. They had obviously decided to take an early morning sail, although judging from the mirror-smoothness of the lake there wouldn't be much wind for sailing.

Turning away, she tried to ignore the feeling of emptiness in the pit of her stomach, trying to blot out the disturbing scene of Rupert and Penelope together. But it was impossible, and all the vague doubts that had been troubling her the past week returned in force, numbing her heart with unhappiness.

Suddenly she looked at the ring on her finger. The diamonds seemed to sparkle coldly in the morning sunlight. Impulsively snatching it from her finger, she held it in the palm of her hand, where it winked back at her with a mocking glitter. Unhappily she wondered what she should do, what could she do? She just didn't understand Rupert, he had wanted their marriage date brought forward, and if he had changed his mind he certainly hadn't mentioned it, although talking to him about anything had been difficult. They never seemed to be alone together.

'You'd better put that back on, you might lose it,' said a quiet voice beside her.

Startled, Abigail looked up. She'd been so engrossed in her thoughts that she hadn't heard Greg cross the patio towards her.

'I . . .' she began.

'Put it on,' he commanded, then added with a wry twist to his lips, 'if you were thinking of throwing it over the edge in a fit of pique, I would advise against it.'

'I am *not*,' said Abigail, 'given to fits of pique!' She put the ring back on her finger.

'You're thinking that Rupert is neglecting you,' began Greg.

'Certainly not,' cut in Abigail quickly—much too quickly, she realised as Greg raised an ironical eyebrowy. 'I didn't know he intended to go sailing this morning, I was just a little surprised.'

Maria appeared in the doorway leading from the villa to the patio, bringing out a tray of fresh bread rolls, which she placed on the breakfast table.

'Come on,' said Greg, taking Abigail's arm, and leading her away from the balustrade. 'This is one advantage of taking a late breakfast, we can have fresh bread, straight from the ovens.'

Abigail walked with him, noticing for the first time how immaculate he looked in cream-coloured slacks and a pale lemon shirt which accentuated his deepening tan. 'You're looking very smart this morning,' she couldn't resist saying. It was true, he usually wore jeans and a T-shirt, the most practical clothes for sailing or sightseeing.

He threw her a thoughtful glance as he said, 'there is a reason, but you've obviously forgotten.'

Abigail frowned. What on earth was he talking about? 'Forgotten what?' she asked.

'The visit to the hospital,' he replied. 'I'm operating at Siena later today, and you're helping me, remember?'

Her hand flew guiltily to her mouth; she had completely forgotten. 'I'd better get ready, she gasped, hastily pushing back her chair.

'Sit down and eat some breakfast first,' he growled, grasping her wrist and dragging her down beside him. Then he grinned wickedly, 'Now you know why your darling fiancé and Penelope have gone sailing for the day, because you'll be otherwise occupied.'

'You told Rupert?'

'Of course. I couldn't very well steal his fiancée for the day without mentioning it, could I?' The remark was innocent enough, but there was a note of hidden laughter in his voice.

Abigail flushed; he was mocking her, laughing at her for removing her engagement ring so impulsively. It seemed a stupid thing to do now that it all made sense. What a jealous, silly woman she had become—she almost laughed

out loud at her own neuroses. Of course Rupert and
Penelope would do something else, if she and Greg were
going to be away all day in Siena.

She took the bread roll he proffered and remained silent
during their breakfast, her mind busily revising the theatre
techniques she had looked up some time before. Gulping
down her coffee, she made her excuses to go and get
changed, even though Greg said there was no hurry. She
wanted to look through the books just once more.

'There won't be too much for you to do,' said Greg,
accurately reading her mind.

'Maybe not,' retorted Abigail, 'but I want to make sure
that what I do is absolutely correct.'

'You worry too much,' laughed Greg, lazily pouring
himself another coffee, 'I've told you so before.'

Abigail didn't answer, just made good her escape to her
room, hastily fishing out the books, and feverishly flicking
through the pages, familiarising herself with the theatre
techniques, although she already knew them backwards.
At the same time, she cursed Greg for not reminding her
before the actual day had arrived!

Changing into the most businesslike outfit she had
brought with her, a blue and white tailored dress, she
carefully pinned her blond hair into a neat chignon, then
hurried down to join Greg in the courtyard. The journey
to Siena took about an hour, and in spite of feeling
apprehensive about the theatre work ahead of her, Abigail
was entranced as usual by the scenery. Monasteries, hilltop
towns perched on rocky crags, all combined with a
kaleidoscope of ever-changing greens and golds into a
timeless landscape.

Greg looked down at her rapt face. 'You looked
bewitched,' he teased.

Abigail smiled. 'Perhaps I am.'

'I'd like to think it was my enthralling company,' he said with a wry smile, 'but I'm inclined to think that it's Italy you're in love with!'

There was no time to continue the conversation, as they had arrived on the outskirts of Siena. The hospital where Greg was to operate was situated in a square just off the Piazza del Campo. Greg had been there before, and negotiated the narrow streets with an expertise born of practice, swinging the car into the hospital's overcrowded parking area without a problem.

As soon as they stepped into the interior of the hospital Greg was greeted with enthusiasm, and Abigail felt at home too; the familiar antiseptic smell, the long shining corridors, the atmosphere of calm ordered efficiency soothed her nerves. She suddenly felt more confident. She would be able to discharge her duties, and do it well; she would be a credit to herself and to Greg.

The two hours' work went well, and Abigail forgot everything else, as Greg snapped orders at her, and she carried out his commands without a moment's hesitation. She also found watching the bloodless laser surgery completely absorbing—the invisible beam of light excising the skin and sealing the blood vessels in one split second. As Greg explained later to his attentive audience, this provided minimum discomfort to the patient during the post-perative period, as the usual oedema associated with major surgery was absent; the laser beam causing little trauma to the surrounding tissues.

After the operating session, they were taken to lunch, where Greg was continually bombarded with questions. Abigail sat quietly eating her lunch, marvelling at Greg's patience. She knew by now he must be feeling tired—two hours of difficult surgery, followed by another two hours of non-stop questioning. At last they made their escape, after many handshakes all round, Abigail only nodding her head and smiling, wishing she could understand the babble of excited conversation.

They had started walking back towards the parked car when Greg paused and looked at his watch. 'We still have time to fit in a little sightseeing,' he said. 'Shall we climb the bell tower in the Piazza del Campo and take in an aerial view of Siena? That is, of course, if you can make it after that lunch!'

'Of course I can make it,' retorted Abigail indignantly, 'I'm very fit.'

'Wait until we come down and then tell me whether or not you're fit,' was the sceptical reply.

Climbing up inside the spiral staircase of the bell tower was more difficult than Abigail had imagined, and she gratefully accepted the offer of Greg's hand to help her up. Once at the top, however, the view of the surrounding Tuscan countryside, and the spectacle of Siena's streets spread out like the spokes of a wheel, made it all worth while.

A group of German tourists, puffing and panting, came squeezing past them to look from the other side of the tower, and Greg drew Abigail in close to make room for them. She was suddenly aware of the uneven hammering of her heartbeat reverberating in her ears, and at the same time she realised that she had not thought of Rupert for a single moment, not since the morning when she'd started out for Siena with Greg. Irritably she turned her head, trying to escape the shadowy image of Rupert, only to find herself looking into the depths of Greg's coal-black eyes. For a fleeting moment, she thought she glimpsed a deep tenderness, but then it was gone, replaced with his usual enigmatic expression.

His head with its mass of dark hair, bent fractionally towards her, and Abigail knew she was almost willing him to kiss her. His face was so close, and yet at the same time a million miles away. She could feel the warmth of his breath on her cheeks, and his lips came closer; then the German tourists came back, noisy and effervescent, bumbling past them, shattering the fragile moment into a thousand pieces.

'We'd better start back down,' said Abigail, watching the retreating back of the noisy crowd, 'it seems to be getting dark already.'

Greg looked at his watch. 'Yes,' he agreed, 'we don't want to miss dinner. I hardly ate any lunch, it was difficult eating pasta *and* fending questions.'

His tone was matter-of-fact and coolly friendly, giving her the uncanny feeling that the moment before the arrival of the Germans had been a figment of her imagination.

During the drive back to the villa, Greg talked casually about the morning's work, and answered some of her questions. She suggested that he should invite Sister Collins into theatre when he returned, to see the 'new-fangled method' as she would still insist on calling it.

'Perhaps I will,' he said, 'although I must confess Sister Collins and the County General seem very far away at the moment.'

'Not so far,' said Abigail pensively. 'We shall be back there next week, and then all this will seem far away.'

'Will you be sorry to leave?' he asked suddenly.

'I've enjoyed my holiday,' she replied warily, choosing her words with care. She didn't want Greg to know that she had been assailed with doubts about Rupert and

Penelope ever since she had arrived in Italy.

But almost as if he could read her innermost thoughts, Greg suddenly said, 'I wonder if Rupert and Penelope had a good sail?'

'I wonder,' replied Abigail.

Then the surprising thought struck her; she wasn't as anxious about Rupert spending his day with Penelope as she should have been. Could it be because she had enjoyed her day with Greg so much? It was a question she couldn't answer, but somehow it didn't seem to matter that much.

Dinner that night was the usual prolonged affair, but Abigail thought Rupert seemed strangely edgy, although no one else appeared to notice, least of all Penelope. She, on the contrary, was in an extra vivacious mood, and regaled everyone with Rupert's prowess at sailing.

'He's such fun to be with,' she said to Abigail. 'He had me in absolute stitches all day.'

Must have worn him out in the process, thought Abigail, glancing at Rupert's tight face, but she didn't allow a flicker of animosity to reach her face, merely saying, 'I'm so glad you had a good day.'

'Did you enjoy yourselves?' Penelope asked without interest, adding, 'personally I can't think of anything more boring than to work when on holiday. Talk about a busman's holiday!'

'It was fascinating,' said Abigail briefly.

Penelope's tinkly little laugh ricocheted around the patio. 'I always knew you were a workaholic,' she said. Then she leaned over to Rupert and took his arm, whispering confidentially, 'You'll have to work on Abigail. You know what they say, all work and no play!'

'I hardly think that applies to Abigail,' muttered Rupert, looking distinctly uncomfortable.

'I don't think Abigail is dull,' said Greg's mother, who had the same disconcerting habit as her son of coming straight to the point.

'Oh, I didn't mean *you* were dull, Abigail,' said Penelope, positively dripping with insincerity, 'I meant that you work much too hard.'

Greg had said nothing at all during this exchange of conversation, just leaned back in his chair, his face in the shadow. Abigail was uneasily aware that he was watching, taking everything in, mulling over the verbal crossfire. She wondered what thoughts were passing through his head; his expression, as usual, gave nothing away.

But as for Rupert, it was quite obvious what was going through *his* head. He was distinctly embarrassed, and Abigail couldn't help mentally smiling. Poor Rupert, Penelope had put him on the spot and he didn't know which way to turn. But one thing she knew, and that was they had to talk, and talk alone. The situation was getting out of hand, Penelope was assuming a proprietorial air over Rupert, and she, Abigail, would have to do something about it.

When the meal had finished, Abigail hung back on the patio, hoping that Rupert would take the hint and stay behind too, but Mrs Lincoln suddenly asked him to take something into the villa, and he quickly agreed. The alacrity with which he acceded to Mrs Lincoln's request made Abigail certain that he had done so in order to avoid being left alone with her. Instead, she found herself alone on the patio with Greg, not the way she had planned it at all.

Inwardly Abigail fumed angrily. Damn! Would she never have the chance to speak to Rupert alone, was she destined to wait until they returned to England before she could speak privately to her own fiancé?

There was nothing to do but wander slowly across the patio and gaze at the view. Leaning on the balustrade, she watched pinpoints of lights out on the lake, small boats fishing. It was late now, even the noisy cicadas were quiet, a soft breeze wafted on the warm night air, lifting the delicate tendrils of hair about her face. Through the purple haze of night, a sparkling galaxy of lights shimmered from the opposite shore of the lake.

'Penny for them?' came Greg's voice at her side.

'I was thinking how lovely the view is,' said Abigail, unable to think of anything better to say.

'My sentiments exactly,' agreed Greg, but looking at her, not the lake, 'although I wasn't thinking of the scenery.'

Almost instinctively she turned towards him. The darkness enveloped them like a warm mantle, as Greg slowly drew her closer. In the intimacy of the night, Abigail raised her face to his, her pulses fluttering wildly to an unfamiliar rhythm. Slowly he bent his head to hers, the heady smell of his skin wafted across her pulsating senses, then his warm lips touched hers briefly.

He drew back. 'Your fiancé is a fool,' he whispered softly. 'He should pay more attention to you, then you wouldn't stray into other men's arms.'

At his words Abigail stiffened. 'I am not straying . . .' she started to say.

'What exactly would you call it, then?'

'I . . . er . . . oh damn you!' Quickly she twisted herself out of his arms, and stood clutching the stone balustrade for support. A girl's legs are only supposed to turn to jelly in books, she thought inconsequentially, not in real life! She glowered at Greg. How was it he made her feel guilty, like some Jezebel? As if she had tempted him, but it had been the other way around—or had it?

The moon sailed on its ribbon of light across the sky, and a shaft of moonlight sliding between the branches of the umbrella pine beside the patio splashed them both in a cold pool of light.

'If you want my opinion, I think Rupert has lost interest,' said Greg abruptly. 'It seems to me he's much more interested in Sir Jason's daughter, and all the business contacts that go with it.'

'I don't want your opinion,' cried Abigail, hurt by his cruel words.

'Maybe not,' said Greg, 'but it's about time you started facing up to the inevitable. If you really want to change things, you'll have to put up a fight.' With that, he abruptly turned on his heel and walked back to the villa.

Abigail stood staring after him, gripping the stonework of the balustrade until her knuckles gleamed white in the moonlight. Hot resentful tears welled up in her eyes. How dared he say cruel, untrue things like that! But a relentless nagging little voice at the back of her mind cried out, It's true, it's true, you know it's true. Rupert is more interested in Penelope than you.

'It is *not* true,' she whispered out loud.

Mentally, she tried to shake her jumbled thoughts into something resembling order; reminding herself that soon she would be back in England, and Rupert would be with her. At the end of September they were to be married, Rupert hadn't called it off, and this time next year Greg Lincoln would be back in America, Penelope would have forgotten Rupert, and all would be well.

She would be settled into a new routine, a life of domesticity as Rupert's wife.

'I shouldn't count on it,' piped up that annoying little voice, unbidden but as devastatingly persistent as ever!

CHAPTER TEN

IT WAS NO use, Abigail reasoned, battling with continually recurring doubts, and when an opportunity presented itself immediately after breakfast the following day, she took it.

'Rupert, let's walk down to the boathouse, we can have a chat,' she said pointedly.

It was not so much a suggestion as a statement, leaving Rupert no option but to agree. Penelope rose to accompany them, but Abigail's expression was one which even she couldn't mistake, and she sat back in her seat wearing a resigned expression.

Once out of earshot of the villa, Abigail came straight to the point. 'We're not going to get married, are we, Rupert?' she heard herself saying. 'We just don't love each other enough.'

The words were out. It hadn't been at all what she had intended to say, but somehow the words spilled out of their own accord.

'I'm very fond of you, Abigail,' began Rupert.

'Fond, yes,' interrupted Abigail, 'but not fond enough to spend much time with me; since I've been here you've spent most of your time with Penelope.'

'You haven't objected too much, since you've spent quite a bit of time with Greg,' observed Rupert, his voice sounding sullen.

A frown creased her forehead. The conversation wasn't going the way she'd planned at all. She hadn't intended to quarrel with Rupert, although she had to admit her opening statement had hardly been conducive to the furtherance of good relations! Rupert fidgeted about, scuffing one foot amongst the loose gravel on the path. He looked very unhappy, and Abigail too felt a sadness overwhelming her. Silently she slipped the ring off her finger and held it out to him.

'I think I'd better return this,' she said quietly.

For a moment he hesitated, then to took the ring and pocketed it. 'I don't know what to say,' he mutterd.

'There isn't much we can say really, is there?' asked Abigail. Suddenly she felt relieved, as if a great weight had been lifted from her shoulders.

'I . . . suppose I might as well come clean,' said Rupert, flushing a dull red. 'I didn't know how to tell you that I wanted to marry Penelope. I told Greg last night—he didn't seem very surprised, though,' he added.

Abigail stood silent. No, she reflected, Greg wouldn't have been at all surprised. Hadn't he said last night that Rupert was more interested in 'Sir Jason's daughter, and all the business contacts that went with her?'

'The only thing is . . .' Rupert hesitated, then said, 'I might as well tell you. I had thought that perhaps Greg cared for you, but somehow I think I put my foot in it badly when I mentioned money.' He turned to face her, his mouth moving convulsively, his eyes troubled. 'He just sort of froze up, but I didn't mean that you were looking for a man with money, I was trying to tell him that I was concerned about you, how you'd manage, with the expenses of the cottage and everything . . .' His voice tailed off lamely.

'Don't worry,' said Abigail drily, 'I'm well aware that Greg thinks I'm after a man for security!' She tried to laugh lightly, but it was a bitter sound that escaped her lips. 'You merely confirmed what he already thought.' She turned, and started to walk back up the path, then paused and looked back. 'Anyway, you're very mistaken in thinking Greg Lincoln cares for me. Attracted slightly, yes, but that's not the same thing. And he is definitely *not* my type!'

'You mean to tell me you and Rupert have broken it off?' demanded Penelope later that afternoon, as they lay sunbathing on the lake shore.

Abigail sat up, hugging her knees to her chest, watching the figures of Rupert and Greg on the small sailing dinghy far out in the middle of the lake.

'I should have thought Rupert would have already told you,' she said quietly.

'He will,' said Penelope with a smug confidence, adding as an afterthought, 'I'm sorry for you, of course, Abigail.'

'Don't be,' said Abigail quickly. 'I feel happier now that it's done.'

'It makes everything so much easier,' mused Penelope.

'What do you mean?'

'Rupert and I are not returning to England with you and Greg on Thursday,' said Penelope. 'He hasn't finished the work here for Daddy, another lucrative contract has come up.'

'But aren't you due back on the ward?' asked Abigail.

Penelope looked momentarily uncomfortable, then brazened it out. 'I've already telephoned in my resignation,' she said airily, 'and a letter is on its way confirming it.'

Abigail spread her hands in a gesture of surprise. It suddenly seemed incredible that she could have been so blind. Although deep in her heart she knew it wasn't so much a case of being blind, rather that she had been purposely wearing blinkers.

'Nursing has never really been my forte,' confessed Penelope, languidly applying suntan oil to her shapely legs.

'I had noticed,' Abigal couldn't help rejoining. 'I'm surprised it's taken you this long to find out!'

The next two days couldn't pass quickly enough as far as Abigail was concerned. Although not a word had passed between the four of them it was by silent mutual consent that the broken engagement was not mentioned to the rest of the household. Of course, Greg's parents knew that only Greg and Abigail were returning to England, but if they thought anything was amiss, they kept their thoughts to themselves.

'The trouble with working in a hospital, dear,' said Greg's mother as she kissed her effusively goodbye, 'is that duty always comes first.'

Abigail smiled. 'Thank you for a lovely holiday, I'm only sorry it's over.' But she couldn't help thinking as she spoke that a part of her life was over too. She'd been right about her premonition of doom at the prospect of visiting Italy.

It was a strange, silent trip back to England. Abigail had expected Greg to refer to her broken engagement, even if only to say 'I told you so'. But he made no mention of it. Even on the drive back from Heathrow, he remained silent, limiting his remarks to brief invectives when someone foolishly cut across lanes on the motorway.

Several times Abigail stole furtive glances at his profile, but it was always the same; stern and forbidding. She wished she could say something to break the stony silence, but her mind was stubbornly blank. All she knew was that with each mile they got nearer to their destination, she felt more depressed and miserable. A fact not helped by gale force winds and lashing rain, which buffeted the car on its journey.

When they finally reached her cottage, Greg helped her in with the luggage. 'I won't stop,' he said, 'I'm tired, and I'm sure you must be too.'

'Yes,' admitted Abigail, looking around at the familiar things spread out in the lounge. It was then that she noticed the damp patch by the chimney breast. Involuntarily she went across and felt the spot; it was damp to her touch. Damn, the pouring rain must have penetrated one of the cracked tiles on the roof.

Greg noticed it too. 'Roof leak,' he said briefly.

'Looks like it,' said Abigail, trying to sound cheerful. 'I'll have to get the roof patched up.'

'How will you afford it?' he asked practically.

'I shall go to Saudi Arabia and work for eighteen months,' said Abigail on the spur of the moment. She knew plenty of girls who had gone out and earned a tax-free fortune, at least a fortune in comparison to English nurses' pay.

'Saudia Arabia!' exclaimed Greg. 'That's a little drastic, isn't it?'

'Drastic perhaps,' said Abigail defensively, her hackles rising at his incredulous tone, 'but very practical. The salary is five times as much as here, and tax-free. I could pay for a new roof and come back with money in my pocket.'

'I don't think it's a good idea at all,' he said brusquely. 'Saudi Arabia is no place for a girl like you.'

'I'm the best judge of that, I'm quite capable of looking after myself.'

'I'll have a coffee before I go,' announced Greg, suddenly changing his mind, and plonking himself down in the middle of the settee.

Abigail looked at him crossly. She couldn't very well refuse; he had just driven her a hundred miles. But she didn't feel like embarking on a long argument over the relative merits on raising money for a leaking roof! So it was with a slightly ungracious air that she went into the kitchen, and clattered the coffee cups, trying, not very successfully, not to worry about the future. Although she had just said it was practical, she wasn't happy with the idea of working in the Middle East, a fact wild horses couldn't have dragged from her in front of Greg.

She stood quite still for a moment, breathing in the atmosphere of the cottage. Perhaps she should be sensible and sell it; after all, her father hadn't known about all the expenses when he'd asked her to keep it; and he'd been a sick man, not capable of thinking rationally. But still, she was reluctant to break that promise.

The coffee made, she carried the tray through to the lounge, to find Greg with his feet up, looking for all the world as if he intended to stay, just as long as it took to change her mind!

Abigail glanced towards him warily, as silently she passed a steaming cup of coffee. 'Sell the cottage,' he said abruptly, coming straight to the point.

'I've no intention of doing that,' replied Abigail stubbornly.

'Why not? It's only a tumbledown flint cottage.'

'It is *not*!' her voice rose angrily, 'it's the most important thing in life to me!'

'I see.' Greg slowly sipped his coffee, surveying her over the rim of his cup. 'Your fiancé has jilted you for another woman, and all you can think about is your precious cottage!'

'You don't understand anything, it's a waste of time talking to you.' Jumping up, she made a move towards the rain-lashed window.

But Greg reached out, and catching her wrist forced her back, to sit beside him on the settee. 'Sit down,' he ordered tersely. 'I feel responsible for the break-up of your engagement, so I feel responsible for you too.'

'There's no need to feel responsible, it had absolutely nothing to do with you.'

'There's not much advice I can give you about your love life,' he began.

'I don't want any advice,' snapped Abigail, 'especially not from you!'

'OK. Let's stick to the problem of the cottage,' he was undeterred. 'Why are you so determined to keep it?'

Abigail stared stonily across the room, the familiar objects swimming in a haze before her troubled gaze. Greg would never understand a promise made to her dying father, he was too practical, he would never let emotions sway his judgement, she was sure of that.

'Well?' he persisted, 'answer me.'

'You wouldn't understand.'

'Try me,' came the response.

Abigail took a deep breath. 'I promised my father when he was ill that I would keep the cottage. But that's not the only reason—I *want* to keep it. It's the only part of my mother and father I have left.'

'That's ridiculous,' said Greg.

'There you are, I *knew* you wouldn't understand,' cried Abigail angrily. 'It *is* a waste of time talking to you.'

'Why don't you let me finish, before you jump down

my throat!'

She maintained a rebellious silence. What did he know about anything! A few short months ago, before he had arrived from America, everything in her life had been calm and ordered—and now——!

'Abigail,' Greg's voice was surprisingly gentle, 'you have your memories of your parents. Nothing can destroy those, they're yours, locked in your mind to cherish for ever. The cottage, although lovely, is only bricks and mortar. It can't be *that* important to you.'

'It is,' said Abigail stubbornly, 'and I've already decided what to do. I shall give in my notice tomorrow, and go and work in Saudia Arabia.'

Greg snorted impatiently. 'You're the most pigheaded female I know,' he said, 'impossible to help.'

'I don't need your help,' said Abigail proudly. She tilted her head defiantly, grey eyes flashing, challenging him to disagree.

'OK, have it your own way,' said Greg abruptly, swinging his legs down from the settee in an impatient movement and nearly tipping her on to the floor in the process. 'I won't detain you any longer, we're both on duty tomorrow.'

A frigid silence reigned as Abigail opened the door for him; for a moment he paused as if about to say something, but then turning up the collar of his coat against the rain, he disappeared into the darkness.

After he'd gone, a chilly mood of desolation settled over her. The warm sunshine and the sparkling blue waters of the lake in Italy might as well have been on another planet, they seemed so remote. Miserably she humped her luggage up the stairs, averting her eyes from the ominous damp patch of the lounge ceiling.

Next day, back on the ward, everyone crowed with envy at the sight of her tan. 'You are lucky,' sighed Sue, looking at Abigail's sun-streaked hair and healthy tan. 'I look so awful, as if I'm dying!' She peered into the changing room mirror, sticking her tongue out at her reflection.

Abigail burst out laughing. Anyone less like dying would be hard to imagine. Sue's flaming red hair, and cream and pink complexion, combined to make her look permanently in the rudest of health.

'The tan will wear off,' Abigail consoled her, as they walked on to the ward together. Sister Collins was at her desk, and gave a perfunctory nod.

'Do you know, I think she actually missed Mr Lincoln,' said Sue as they pulled the drug trolley out from its corner. 'Even though we didn't have a ward round, she made us all do everything as usual, almost as if she was expecting him to turn up!'

Abigail laughed again. She was feeling better already. She was back in the environment she loved, the hospital. This was where she belonged. They stopped at the first patient, and Abigail poured out the linctus prescribed for Mr Grover, then passed the beaker to Sue. She couldn't help noticing Sue's eyes were riveted on her hand. The ring was gone, but the telltale patch of pale skin showed where it had been.

'Where's your ring?' asked Sue as soon as they had moved away from Mr Grover.

Abigail groaned, but braced herself. Might as well get it over with, everyone would know soon enough anyway. 'I'm no longer engaged,' she answered briefly.

'Oh,' Sue's eyes nearly popped out of her head, 'but it was such a lovely ring!'

'It wasn't the ring I didn't like, it was the prospect of marriage.' She didn't mention Penelope Orchard's involvement—time enough for that juicy piece of gossip to be digested later!

'Oh,' said Sue again, dying to ask more questions. But Abigail's expression didn't encourage her, so she had to contain her curiosity and continue with the drug round.

The rest of the morning dragged. The ward was still half empty from the holidays, and Greg didn't put in an appearance as his patients had yet to be admitted. At lunchtime Abigail hurried down to the canteen, hoping that Lynne might be on the same lunch break as herself. She was in luck, Lynne was sitting alone at a table by the window, and grabbing a salad from the cold counter, Abigail joined her friend.

Lynne looked her up and down enviously, 'It's disgusting,' she said, 'for anyone to be so brown, especially in this weather!' She looked gloomily out of the window, where the rain was still pouring down. 'I got your card, by the way—was it really as lovely as you described it?'

'Better,' said Abigail, the blue skies of Italy flashing momentarily before her eyes, banishing the cold grey of the English summer. 'You must go to Italy some time.'

'Perhaps I will, soon,' said Lynne, suddenly stretching her left hand towards Abigail. A solitaire diamond sparkled on her ring finger. 'We got engaged last weekend,' she breathed. 'Derek doesn't want a long engagement, so we're to be married next month, and he says we might go to Italy for our honeymoon.' The information was imparted in Lynne's usual fashion, without a pause for breath.

'Lynne!' Abigail grasped her friend's hand, 'I'm so

glad.' Then she smiled. 'But I'm not exactly surprised, I can recognise true love when I see it.'

Lynne's face clouded over. 'I hear via the grapevine that you've broken off your engagement to Rupert.'

'Yes,' said Abigail briefly.

'What went wrong?' asked her friend with genuine concern.

Abigail smiled sadly. Seeing Lynne so happy made her feel even more alone. 'It was never really right, Lynne,' she said at last. 'I suppose, deep down, I knew that all the time, but I kidded myself.' Then she made a determined effort and smiled cheerfully. 'At least we didn't make the mistake of getting married and then finding out.' Then she told Lynne, feeling she had to tell someone, that Rupert had fallen for Penelope Orchard.

'Well, of all the nasty creatures!' exploded Lynne.

'It takes two,' Abigail reminded her.

Lynne looked thoughtful. 'On holiday at Greg's villa!' A scheming expression flickered with sudden delight across her face. 'Perhaps you and Greg . . .'

'Forget it,' said Abigail sharply. 'I've had quite enough "romance" to last me for a while. I am definitely *off* men!'

Lynne tactfully changed the subject. 'Your ward busy?'

'Not today, but from tomorrow onwards the workload is going to be very busy, especially for the surgeons. They've called in so many patients it isn't true.'

Lynne laughed. 'That makes me even more glad I'm going to marry a radiologist. At least he'll be home sometimes to see his children growing up.' She peered across at Abigail's watch hanging from her uniform pocket. 'Heavens, is that the time? I must dash—see you.' Snatching up her tray, she scurried away.

Left on her own, Abigail sat watching the raindrops

sliding relentlessly down the windowpane; it really was foul weather, grey and cheerless, not summer at all. Fits my mood, she thought dejectedly.

She walked slowly back to the ward, wishing it was tomorrow when they would be busy; if there was one thing she hated it was inactivity. But as soon as she arrived Sister Collins called her over.

'Staff,' she said, 'I've volunteered you to help on the children's section, they're rather busy round there. I hope you don't mind, but as you've not had a lot of experience with children, I thought it would stand you in good stead when you apply for a Sister's post.'

'Why, thank you,' said Abigail, glad to have something positive to do; although as far as helping her with an application for a Sister's post—well, that was another matter. In fact, it was something she hadn't thought of terribly seriously.

As she walked to the children's section she mulled the idea over, but then rejected it. Even a Sister's salary wouldn't be enough to pay for the repairs to the cottage; there was nothing for it but Saudi Arabia. Although in spite of her defiant words to Greg the previous evening, she'd put off handing in her notice that day.

Once she arrived on the children's section, however, her own problems were forgotten. 'Thank goodness you've come!' cried Sister Moon when she spied her. 'We've got every bed full, and the problem is they're all feeling well!'

That fact was not difficult to deduce, judging from the racket emanating from a room down the corridor.

'Would you believe it, but that's the *quiet* room!' said Sister Moon, agitatedly pushing back stray strands of hair beneath her cap. 'I've had to let them overflow from the activity room.'

Abigail raised her eyebrows. 'Sounds as if there's plenty of activity going on in the quiet room,' she observed with a smile.

Sister Moon agreed. 'The trouble is our play leader is sick. I need someone to help with their drawing and painting—do you think you can do it?'

'I'll try anything once,' replied Abigail, and set off down the corridor in the direction of the noise.

Surprising even herself, she found it easy to entertain the children. Casting her mind back to her own infant days, she showed them how to cut up potatoes and make potato prints. In no time at all peace reigned, as the children busily printed their potato pictures on large sheets of coloured paper.

'Can we hang them up when they're finished?' demanded one small boy with an attractive husky voice.

'Yes,' said Abigail, hoping Sister Moon wouldn't object to the corridor being festooned with coloured paper.

So intent was she, kneeling on the floor helping a little girl press down her potato firmly, that she didn't hear Sister Moon and Greg Lincoln come in.

'Ah, peace at last! Well done, Nurse Pointer.' At the sound of Sister Moon's voice Abigail turned.

They were standing in the doorway of the quiet room, which by now was living up to its name. Greg was smiling, and involuntarily Abigail found herself smiling back; the dancing light in his sparkling brown eyes was quite infectious.

'You have a blue blob on the end of your nose,' he remarked, adding as Abigail vainly rubbed at it, 'Now you've added red—a most becoming combination!'

Greg and Sister Moon left, and Abigail turned back to the children. Her spirits had lifted, and as if to complement her feelings, the rain stopped and the sun came out, its warming rays sloping through the windows of the quiet room. The afternoon had passed by quickly, so absorbed had she been with her work with the children.

'I think we'd better clean these children up and get them back into bed now,' she told the student nurse helping her. 'Supper will be coming round soon.'

'Don't forget you said you'd pin up our pictures,' reminded the husky-voiced boy with a disarming smile, whose name Abigail had found out was Timmy Smith.

Good as her word, Abigail clambered on a chair and dutifully pinned up the pictures in the corridor. Then it was a rush, getting the children washed before supper time.

'It's fish fingers tonight,' said Timmy Smith, 'my favourite.' He smiled up at her, and Abigail was struck one again by the unselfconscious charm of the little boy.

Making her way down the staircase much later, when she had finally finished, she suddenly realised just how tired she felt. From being bored in the morning, she had been completely absorbed all the afternoon, so it was only now that she felt tired.

'You look weary.' It was Greg, flying down the stairs two at a time. 'Did all those children exhaust you?'

'A little,' Abigail admitted, 'but I enjoyed myself.'

'I could see that,' he returned drily. 'Didn't I tell you I could imagine you surrounded by hordes of children!'

She blushed. 'If I ever do have children,' she said lightly, 'it will never be that many!'

'Thought any more about Saudi Arabia?' he asked suddenly, changing the subject.

'Yes,' said Abigail.

'Don't rush into anything you might regret . . .'

'Don't worry,' she interrupted with just a trace of bitterness, 'I've learned my lesson. I'm not going to rush into anything.'

'Good,' said Greg briskly, 'at least that's an improvement on last night's attitude!' Then he stopped, and leaning forward lightly touched the tip of her nose with his forefinger. 'It's still red and blue,' he said with a grin, 'did you forget?' Then he carried on his way, down the stairs two at a time, and disappeared through the swing doors at the bottom.

CHAPTER ELEVEN

IT WAS well into the next day before Abigail had a spare moment in which to sit down at the nursing station and scan the *Nursing Mirror* for jobs in Saudi Arabia. She still hadn't been able to bring herself to actually hand in her notice, thinking, I'll get some job descriptions first, then give in my notice. Out of the corner of her eye, she saw Sister Collins approaching, and hastily stuck the journal in the nearest drawer. She could just imagine Sister's horrified reaction if she knew Abigail was even contemplating such a move.

'I'm off to my meeting now,' said Sister Collins, 'but I wondered if I could ask you a favour before I go, it's important I get it settled now. Are you doing anything special tonight?'

'No,' said Abigail truthfully, instinctively knowing she was going to be asked to do extra duty.

She was right! 'Good,' said Sister Collins, sounding relieved. 'I know I always seem to ask you, but you're one of my most reliable girls. Could you work until nine o'clock tonight? I know it means a very long day,' she added hurriedly, 'but it's imperative I get someone good for Mary Mulligan, the post-operative laser patient.'

'The girl who's having her trachy closed today?'

'Yes. Mr Lincoln asked that someone senior keep an eye on her.' Abigail agreed, she knew of the case and had been on duty when Mary had first been brought in earlier in the year as a result of a road traffic accident. The pretty teenager's larynx had been damaged, necessitating a tracheostomy, and now it was to be closed, always a hazardous procedure. Sister Collins went off to her meeting happy in the knowledge that Abigail was staying, and as for herself—well, Abigail thought philosophically, working was better than going home and worrying about the roof! She also decided that procrastination was not the answer, so she penned a letter to a nursing agency which dealt with Middle Eastern jobs, dropping the envelope into the post porter's basket before she had a chance to change her mind.

Once the afternoon theatre patients starting arriving back on the ward from Recovery, all thoughts of Saudi Arabia, and the cottage, were driven from her mind. There was so much to do, and she was hard-pushed to keep pace with everything; she had Sue Parkins and another student nurse on loan, and kept them on the run following her instructions. But although both girls were willing, the bulk of the work fell on Abigail's shoulders, because as students neither of them were qualified to administer the drugs written up by the anaesthetist.

'Would you like me to stay on for a bit?' volunteered Sue, when the time came for her to go off duty.

Abigail smiled gratefully at Sue's generous offer, knowing she had a date that evening with a houseman she had been idolising from afar for weeks. 'It will quieten down now,' she replied, 'it's only a question of the top-ups. I shall manage. But thanks for the offer.'

'Sure?' asked Sue.

'Quite sure,' said Abigail firmly. 'Now off you go, or you'll be late for your date tonight.'

Sue blushed to the roots of her flaming red hair, then shot off down the corridor at express train speed, towards the changing room.

Once Sue had gone, Abigail briefed the new auxiliary, a pleasant willing girl named Ann. They had just finished the drug round for the post-operative patients, checking that the analgesics were working well, and that the patients were pain-free, when Greg strode into the ward.

'Shouldn't you be off duty?' he asked, looking surprised to find Abigail still there.

'We're short-staffed,' she explained. 'I'm staying until nine o'clock, mainly for Mary Mulligan's benefit. Sister Clarkson comes on then, so there'll be no problem.'

He seemed relieved. 'Good,' he muttered absentmindedly, and went across to Mary's room just opposite the nursing station. He stood, one hand lightly holding the girl's wrist as he felt her pulse. The closure of tracheostomy had to all intents and purposes gone well, but Abigail could see that he was worried.

'She seems to be doing well,' she ventured.

'Yes,' he muttered, but he still looked worried. 'Let her have something cold to drink now, I'll be back later to check her out. Keep a very close watch on her breathing.'

'Do you anticipate problems?' asked Abigail quietly, as together they walked away from Mary's room.

He waited until they reached the nursing station before replying, 'I wasn't able to laser the closure as well as I would have liked,' he said briefly. 'My main concern is that oedema will develop.'

Abigail noticed his face was sallow with concern, taut lines etched deeply into the corners of his mouth. Impulsively she reached out and caught his arm. 'Don't worry,' she said, 'I'll watch her carefully and call the duty doctor if I'm the slightest bit worried.'

'No,' he snapped, 'don't call him, call me. Switch can

get me through my radio pager.' He turned abruptly, and walked quickly down the corridor leading away from the ward.

Abigail watched until he was out of sight. He was particularly touchy, even for him, she mused. Then she went back into Mary's room, and was rewarded by a weak smile from the seventeen-year-old. 'You can have a cold drink now,' she said, 'it will help soothe your throat.'

Mary nodded. 'That would be nice,' she whispered hoarsely.

She sipped the ice-cold milk Abigail had prepared gratefully. The hand that held the glass was steady, no sign of tremor, but when she began to swallow Abigail felt a twinge of anxiety. Mary was quite happy, but Abigail noted that the milk seemed to gurgle down rather slowly, rather than slip down easily the way it should have done.

'How does it feel when you're drinking?' she asked in a matter-of-fact voice. The very last thing she wanted was to convey any hint of anxiety to Mary.

'Fine,' whispered Mary, 'the milk is lovely.'

Abigail mentally chastised herself for looking for problems where there were none; Greg had made her nervous. She waited until Mary had finished, then twitched the pillows into a more comfortable position and settled her down. She stood and watched as Mary drifted off easily to sleep, then, satisfied that all was well, left her bedside.

The evening shift passed quickly, and Abigail checked on Mary every five to seven minutes, and couldn't help wishing she was out in the main ward instead of in an individual room, even though it was near the nursing station. Give me the old-fashioned wards any time, she thought, when it was possible to see all the patients at a glance from the central desk. Ann went off for her tea break, and returned just as some visiting relatives stopped at the desk to ask Abigail some questions.

'Pop in and check on Mary, will you?' asked Abigail. Five minutes had passed since she herself had checked and all had been well. Ann nodded and disappeared into Mary's room, only to reappear a second later and hurry over to the desk, her face ashen.

'Staff!' she called, rushing to Abigail's side.

'Don't run, nurse,' snapped Abigail, only too aware of the audience of anxious relatives. 'You know you must never run on the ward.'

She rose quickly, excusing herself to the relatives in a calm voice, although her thoughts were racing ahead, sifting through all the possible disasters. 'What is it?' she asked, keeping her voice low.

'She's not breathing properly!' gasped Ann, panic rising in her voice. 'I think she's dying!'

'Not if I can help it,' rejoined Abigail grimly, pushing open the door to Mary's room. One glimpse was enough to tell her something was terribly wrong.

'Call the crash team,' she said without hesitation. Mary's pulse was weak and fluttering, her breathing laboured, and Abigail noted peripheral cyanosis. She knew the girl was about to arrest any moment—but why? Why? Then she noticed Mary's fingers, feebly plucking at the dressing covering the site of the operation, and Greg's words came back to Abigail with harrowing clarity. 'My main concern is that oedema will develop.' Suddenly she knew Greg's fear had been realised, and there was only one solution—the tracheostomy would have to be re-opened quickly.

'The crash team are in Casualty with a coronary case,'

said Ann, putting down the telephone.

'Tell Switch to get the other team and also to page Mr Lincoln, urgently. Then come and help me,' said Abigail, running from Mary's room to the utility room, her previous adminition about running forgotten. There were times when a nurse *had* to run, and this was one of them. So she ran, unmindful of the puzzled stares of the remaining visitors as they wended their way from the ward. She grabbed the trolley which stood equipped, ready for such emergencies, and wheeled it into Mary's room.

There was still no sign of a doctor. 'Where are they?' Abigail asked Ann, who was standing looking panic-stricken, wringing her hands.

'They're on their way,' she said, her voice trembling.

'We can't wait,' said Abigail tersely, her mind racing ahead, planning each move she was about to make with meticulous detail. She looked at Ann. 'Just give me what I ask for, and everything will be all right.' She spoke calmly and quietly, knowing what she had to do. She nodded towards the piped oxygen supply by the side of the bed. 'Have the oxygen ready, and give it to me the moment I ask for it, and pass me this tube when I give the word.'

She handed Ann a tracheostomy tube and leaned over Mary. Please let me be doing the right thing, she prayed silently, cold beads of perspiration breaking out on her brow. Then taking a deep breath she started carefully to snip open the sutures that were keeping the tracheostomy closed. The senior house officer, Dr Singh, came in.

'What—?' he began.

'Oedema in the larynx,' said Abigail briefly, snipping away at the sutures. 'Do you want to take over?'

'No,' he said quickly, 'don't stop now.'

So Abigail carried on, knowing there was not a minute

to be lost, although it was as much as she could do to keep
her hands steady. Only when the airway had been opened,
the tracheostomy tube inserted, and life-giving pure
oxygen was flowing into Mary's lungs, did she stand back.

'You saved her life,' said Dr Singh in an awed voice,
standing by Mary feeling her pulse and noting the colour
of her face, which was rapidly improving.

Suddenly the enormity of what she had done, and what
could have gone wrong, struck Abigail; at that point the
crash team burst into the room, closely followed by Greg.

'What's going on?' he demanded, marching up to
Mary's bedside.

'Staff Nurse Pointer seems to have made us all
redundant,' said the anaesthetist, busily checking the
oxygen flow to the now peaceful Mary, as Dr Singh filled
him in on the details.

Startled, Greg flashed Abigail a questioning look, but
she was incapable of answering, the full horror of what
might of happened overwhelming her.

'Take Staff and get her some strong coffee,' he ordered
brusquely, nodding his head towards Ann.

The young auxiliary touched Abigail's arm, and on legs
that could scarcely function properly, she walked silently
out of the room, hoping that Greg wouldn't be angry
because she had gone ahead and re-opened the
tracheostomy. The tone of his voice had been very abrupt.
Perhaps she should have waited for the medical team to
arrive.

Once outside Mary's room, she became aware of the
excited buzz of conversation throughout the ward area,
and realised all the other patients must be wondering what
was going on.

She took a deep breath. It was ridiculous to tremble now

it was all over. 'I'll get myself a coffee,' she told Ann. 'You go and do a routine ward check. If anyone asks what's been going on, just say there was a slight problem, but all is now well.'

Ann pulled a face. 'A bit of an understatement!' But she knew well enough that it was essential not to worry the other patients.

Once in the ward kitchen, Abigail made a coffee automatically, pondering over the events of a short while ago. She was sure she had done the right thing, but Greg Lincoln hadn't exactly congratulated her, she remembered with a little pang.

'I've come to thank you,' Greg's deep voice cut through her thoughts, almost as if he knew her doubts, 'and to congratulate you on your expertise.'

'Congratulate me . . .?' stammered Abigail.

'Yes. If you hadn't made the correct diagnosis and responded immediately, Mary Mulligan would no longer be with us.'

Inexplicably Abigail's eyes filled with tears, and the hand that held the coffee cup trembled violently. 'I knew I daren't wait for you to arrive,' she whispered in a barely audible voice.'

The coffee cup was promptly taken from her, and suddenly Greg's arms were around her, holding her comfortingly. 'Why is it women always cry when things go right?' he asked whimsically.

Abigail raised her eyes, tears trembling on the edges of her long lashes, 'I don't know, I . . .' His lips came down on hers, in a gentle, softly reassuring kiss.

'All I can say,' he murmured, 'is that you'll be wasted in Saudi Arabia. We need you here.' Then as suddenly as he had taken her in his arms, he released her, and left the kitchen.

Slowly Abigail raised her hands and touched her lips. Did he mean the hospital needed her, or did he mean that he needed her too? She wished she knew.

When she eventually arrived back at the cottage that night, it was about ten, but in spite of being tired she decided to finish her unpacking. She was still too het up to sleep, so she reasoned she might as well do something useful.

The presents and souvenirs she had bought were unwrapped, and she found herself reliving the moment she had purchased each one. She could almost smell the dry dusty smell of the heat around the villa, always mixed with the smell of the wild rosemary which grew in profusion on the hillsides of Umbria. Smiling at the memory, she wondered what Greg's parents were doing; probably sitting outside under the stars, with a glass of wine, she decided enviously. Then she began to wonder why Greg had bought the villa and the land, when he would be returning to America the following year. He would hardly ever have time to go there himself. But perhaps he would settle in England, and not go back, and maybe it was possible that something could come of their relationship, maybe . . .

She shook her head. Stop daydreaming, she told herself firmly. Just because he kissed you by way of saying thank you, it doesn't mean that he likes you. He's probably still feeling sorry for you, poor little Staff Nurse Pointer, ditched by her fiancé for a better catch!

Walking across the bedroom, she stared at her reflection in the mirror. Pale tawny golden hair, grey eyes fringed with dark lashes. Quite a nice face, she thought dispassionately, but not exciting. Not the sort of girl a clever, ambitious man like Greg Lincoln would want to settle down with. He'd flirted with her, that was true, but only when she was safely engaged. Ever since she'd been free he'd shown no interest whatsoever! It's because I'm not exciting, she thought with a sudden surge of irritation at herself. I'm not witty, or ambitious, I'm ordinary, just plain ordinary.

She glowered in the mirror, 'You are dull, dull, dull,' she said, challenging her reflection to contradict her.

The telephone ringing in the hall brought a welcome interruption to her relentless and unflattering self-analysis; hastily she hurried down the stairs to answer it.

'Abigail!' It was Greg, and her heart gave a sudden gigantic flip, as she remembered his kiss of not so long ago. Although why she should remember such a brief, passionless kiss was beyond reason.

However, the memory made her feel suddenly shy, and she answered rather abruptly, 'Yes?'

He hesitated a moment, as if put off by her abruptness, then said, 'I rang to tell you Mary Mulligan is one hundred per cent better. I've talked to her, and she's resigned to the fact of living with her trachy for some time to come.'

'Oh, I'm glad she's OK.' There was a long pause, Abigail couldn't think of anything to say.

Then Greg suddenly said, 'I took some letters down to the post room.'

'And?' She didn't get the connection.

'I saw a handwritten envelope, your handwriting to . . .'

'Oh!' now Abigail knew what was coming, 'you mean the one to the Middle Eastern Agency.'

'It's a stupid idea, don't go ahead with it.'

'Are you telling me, or just giving me advice?' she asked, a hint of irony in her voice. Why was it men always thought they knew best! 'Because as I told you before, I shall do whatever I think fit.'

'I know you will,' Greg's tone was definitely cool, 'I was merely voicing an opinion. For your own good.'

'Thank you, but keep it to yourself.' Abigail could hardly recognise her own voice, it sounded so hard and distant. 'I really don't feel in the slightest bit like taking advice from anyone.'

'Of course,' Greg's voice sounded equally hard and uncompromising, 'I quite understand.' The line went dead and Abigail was left standing in the hall, miserably clutching the receiver to her chest.

Why had she been so stupidly pigheaded? That had been a heaven-sent opportunity to talk, to get to know Greg better, to continue the fragile threads of their relationship, and maybe to clear up some misunderstandings. But all she had done was to make matters worse! Slamming the phone back in its cradle, she sighed. She felt exhausted now, and depressed, and it didn't help knowing that she had been less than reasonable!

Dispiritedly she went back upstairs and finished the unpacking. This time she didn't dawdle, didn't waste time on memories; even so, it was very late by the time she had finished.

The rain was still pouring down heavily outside, and only served to add to her gloom. It made her even more uncomfortably aware that she would have to do something about the roof soon. Pouring herself a glass of red wine from a bottle given her by Greg's father, she took the wine and some cheese and biscuits to the lounge. The light from the fringed lamp by the stone fireplace cast a warm glow over the room as she sat lost in thought. Greg's words came back to her: 'The cottage is only bricks and mortar, nothing can destroy your memories.'

In spite of giving Greg an impression to the contrary, she knew what she had to do; she must sell the cottage. Somebody would buy it who could afford the upkeep, and they would love it as much as she did. Surprisingly, once she had made the decision she felt much better. Where she would live, and what she would do in the future, she pushed to the back of her mind. Let the future take care of itself, she thought bravely.

CHAPTER TWELVE

BEFORE she went on duty the following morning, Abigail rang the Estate Agent and made an appointment to see him in her lunch hour; she did it early just to make certain she didn't get cold feet and back down on her resolve of the night before.

Of course, the ward was buzzing with the story of her dramatic action of the previous night, and as soon as she appeared Sister Collins sent Abigail in to see Mary.

'You are one visitor she will *definitely* want to see,' she said, smiling broadly.

Mary was sitting up in bed, looking healthily pink. She smiled, then pulling a rueful face pointed to her trachy.

'You'll have it closed later,' Abigail comforted her; it was obviously a little bit too soon.

Mary nodded and squeezed Abigail's hand, while her eyes said thank you. Abigail smiled back down at her, a warm glow of satisfaction spreading through her; it was a good feeling to know that Mary was alive, and that she had helped. Special moments like this make everything worthwhile, she thought as she left to carry on with the more mundane aspects of the morning's work.

It was a busy morning, quite a few new admissions, and when lunchtime came she was in such a hurry to keep her appointment with the Estate Agent that she didn't notice Greg come on to the ward as she went flying off in the opposite direction. She had confided in Sister Collins about selling the cottage, asking if she could take her lunch hour between twelve and one.

The Estate Agent assured her that selling the cottage would not be difficult. 'A lot of people from London are buying these cottages as weekend retreats, he told her.

'But I don't want it to be a weekend retreat,' protested Abigail, 'I want it to be someone's home.'

The Estate Agent looked at her in surprise. 'You want the money, don't you?' he asked, 'You'll have to take whoever offers the best price.'

'I suppose you're right,' Abigail agreed reluctantly, privately making up her mind to put off any would-be buyers she didn't like the look of.

She also managed to squeeze in a visit to the Residence Officer of the hospital, during her lunch hour. He was very helpful. She could have a hospital room if the cottage was sold quickly and she needed temporary accommodation while looking for somewhere else. What to do with all the furniture was another problem, and one she shelved for the time being.

The rest of the afternoon didn't allow her to worry about her actions. Dr Singh, their efficient Senior House Officer, had started his holiday, and they had a locum, a tall, gangling fellow, who took everything at one pace, dead slow! You're not going to go down well with your consultant, thought Abigail as she tried to impress upon him that there was some urgency about clerking in the patients!

Because of his lethargy, it was well past her off-duty time before she finished, and then on impulse she went round to the children's section, wanting to see how her charges of the painting session were faring.

She arrived on the section to find Sister Moon at her desk, looking very drawn and sad, not at all like her usual cheerful self.

'What is it?' asked Abigail.

Sister Moon's eyes were full of tears, a fact which was very noticeable as she wore thick glasses which had the effect of magnifying her eyes. 'I'm all right,' she said quickly, and bending down fished a tissue out of the drawer and wiped her eyes. 'Not the way for a Sister to behave,' she added, trying to smile.

'I'm sorry,' said Abigail. 'Is there anything I can do?'

'No,' replied Sister Moon, not bothering to hide the bitterness in her voice, 'there's nothing you can do, nothing even Mr Lincoln can do. It's so unfair—their only child too.'

'Who?'

'Timmy Smith.'

'I remember him,' said Abigail, a feeling of apprehension sweeping over her, 'a lovely little boy, a real charmer.'

'Yes, that's him,' said Sister Moon dully, 'Mr Lincoln did a biopsy this morning, and the result has just come back. Cancer of the larynx.'

Abigail drew in her breath sharply. 'But he's so young!' she exclaimed. 'I didn't think children . . .'

'It's rare,' said Sister Moon, 'but when it happens it's fast growing, and he has the most malignant type possible.' She wiped her streaming eyes again. 'Mr Lincoln is with the parents now. He has to tell them there's nothing anyone can do.'

Abigail felt a cold, hard lump in her throat. 'How awful!' she whispered. It made all her problems seem silly and frivolous. She couldn't think of anything worse than to be told your child was going to die. She turned and walked away. There was nothing she could do, and her heart went out the the parents of Timmy and to Greg, the bearer of such tragic news.

It was a subdued Abigail who went home. The sale of the cottage seemed unimportant. It's true, she thought, looking around at the living room; it *is* only bricks and mortar, people are much more important.

Halfway through her preparations for supper, there was a knock on the door. Startled, she went to answer it. She wasn't expecting anyone, but thought maybe it was Lynne. But it wasn't Lynne, it was Greg, standing in the small brick porch, his huge frame filling up every available inch of space.

'Can I come in?' he asked without preamble.

For an answer Abigail swung the front door open wide and he walked past her without a word through into the lounge. Taking off his jacket, he threw it across one of the chairs, then sank into the deeply cushioned settee. Strain and sorrow were etched deeply into his face, giving him a vulnerable look. His dark eyes were dull, and full of pain.

Without speaking Abigail went into the kitchen and poured him a glass of wine. Taking it through into the lounge, she placed it in his hand.

Wearily Greg raised his eyes to hers. 'I could do with something stronger than this,' he said, looking at the red wine.

Impulsively Abigail sat down beside him and touched his arm. 'Drink it,' she said. 'It's your father's wine, perhaps some of the Italian sunshine will seep into your heart.'

He gave a short laugh. 'What an incurably romantic thing to say!' he said. 'It's the kind of remark my mother would come out with.' Then he continued sombrely, 'I understand from Sister Moon that you came round to the children's section this evening.'

'Yes,' said Abigail slowly, 'she told me about Timmy Smith.' She saw Greg wince at her words, as if in physical pain. 'How did his parents take it?' she asked at last.

'Hard,' said Greg, his voice breaking, 'and I couldn't make it any easier for them. Oh, Abigail, sometimes life is so rotten!'

In one swift movement he was in her arms. She held him as she would a small child, stroking his dark hair with tender hands and gently kissing the top of his head. For a long time they stayed like that, he taking comfort from her encircling arms, she only too happy to give him what he needed most at that time, someone to be with, someone to share his sorrow.

At last he drew away. 'Thank you,' he said simply. Then he gave a lopsided grin. 'Men are supposed to be the stronger sex,' he said, 'not supposed to need comforting.'

'It would be a very hard man, one without a heart, who never needed comfort,' said Abigail gently. Then she got up. 'Have you eaten?' Greg shook his head. 'How about steak and salad, followed by cheese?'

'Sounds like the food of the Gods to me,' said Greg wearily.

They had a late, leisurely supper. Neither of them talked much, somehow it wasn't necessary. It wasn't an awkward or difficult silence, but a companionable one.

When they had finished Abigail carried the dishes through to the kitchen, intending to make some coffee. But when she returned to collect the glasses, Greg was sound asleep on the settee.

Tenderly she looked at his long form lying stretched out in sleep, his dark hair falling, as usual, across his brow. Slowly, as she studied his face, the tender sensuous mouth, the firm jawline that hinted at his determined strength, she realised that without even being aware of it, she had fallen in love with the man now lying exhausted in her lounge. Life is strange, she mused, as she shyly reached out and touched his hair, wondering whether to leave him to sleep, or send him on his way.

Eventually deciding it would be kinder to leave him, she fetched a warm blanket and gently tucked it around him. Then switching off the lights she made her way silently upstairs and went to bed herself.

'Tea!' Startled, Abigail sat bolt upright in bed, to be confronted by Greg standing in front of her with a cup of tea in his hand. 'Tea,' he repeated.

Suddenly aware that she was wearing only the flimsiest of nightdresses, Abigail pulled the sheet up beneath her chin.

Greg laughed. 'Don't be so modest,' he said, 'I've seen more of you in your bikini?'

That was true, of course, but somehow Abigail felt more selfconscious sitting in bed in a nightdress than sitting in a scanty bikini by the side of a swimming pool. 'It isn't quite the same,' she muttered.

'You're right, it isn't,' he agreed, passing her the tea. He paused, looking down at her, a teasing glint in his eyes. 'I'd like to stay,' he said, 'but I can't. I've got a full day's operating starting in one hour. Goodbye, and thanks for everything.' Swiftly he strode out of the bedroom, and quietly closed the door.

Abigail sat in bed, sipping the tea, listening until the noise of his car had died away in the distance. She felt a warm glow inside her, which stayed with her the rest of the morning, in spite of having to cope with two lazy porters, and the locum SHO; between them they constituted a disastrous trio.

Sister asked her to take a late lunch that day, which meant she was alone on the ward for nearly an hour, but as it coincided with a break in theatres there were no post-operative patients to worry about. The ward was peaceful, patients enjoying their lunches, and Abigail took the opportunity to sit and rest at Sister Collins' desk.

The ward phone rang, and Abigail picked it up. 'ENT Ward, Staff Nurse Pointer speaking.'

'Ah, Nurse Pointer,' it was the man from the Estate Agent's. 'Forgive me for ringing you at work, but I thought you'd like to know straight away.'

'Know what?' asked Abigail. Surely the cottage hadn't been sold already!

'We've sold the cottage for you, and at the asking price.'

'But nobody's been to see it,' stammered Abigail, not prepared for such a sudden turn of events. 'How could you have sold it?'

'We have,' the Estate Agent assured her. 'The customer has just been in, paid a handsome deposit and signed the necessary documents.'

'But what about viewing, and a survey?' asked Abigail.

'Not necessary,' he informed her. 'I did suggest it, of course, but the purchaser was adamant—he wants the cottage, doesn't need to see it and doesn't want a survey. What's more, it will be a cash sale, no waiting about for mortgages or anything tiresome like that.'

Abigail was stunned. She hadn't been prepared for the cottage to be sold so quickly. In her heart of hearts, she'd secretly hoped it would stay on the market for ages, even though she hadn't actually admitted that fact to herself.

'Are you still there, Nurse Pointer?' asked the voice at the other end of the line.

'Yes, I'm still here,' said Abigail faintly. 'Thank you for ringing me.' She put the phone down, feeling numb inside; her previous glow evaporating suddenly into a mood of dejection. Don't be stupid, you'll get over it, she told herself sensibly. It has to be done, you should be pleased it's happened so quickly. But she wasn't pleased, she felt too miserable for words.

That evening when she returned to the cottage, she just couldn't settle down. She wandered around the cottage, fingering every beloved thing, and all the memories of her childhood came flooding back with heartrending clarity. It was no use telling herself she couldn't spend her life looking backwards, because her heart wouldn't listen. She went into the kitchen and poured herself a glass of wine, then slumped down at the table, the wine untouched. Burying her head in her arms, she sobbed uncontrollably.

'Been hitting the bottle, I see,' Greg's voice cut through her noisy sobs.

Abigail raised a tear-stained face. 'How did you . . .?'

'Get in?' Greg finished for her. Then he grinned wickedly. 'I took the precaution of taking one of your front door keys on my way out this morning,' he said, waving it under her nose. 'You really should be more careful who you invite in, you know. There are all sorts of undesirable characters about!' He slipped the key back in his pocket.

'But I . . . you . . .' sniffed Abigail, vainly searching for a handkerchief with which to wipe her eyes.

'Come here,' said Greg, passing her a handkerchief and pulling her into his arms at the same time. 'Why are you crying?'

'Because I've made a decision,' her voice was muffled by the handkerchief, 'and now it's done, I'm glad,' she added defiantly.

'I'd hate to see you if you weren't glad!' said Greg, raising his eyebrows.

'I'm glad, but I'm miserable!' wailed Abigail, bursting into tears again, and burying her head on his chest.

'Hold on,' said Greg. 'Abigail, your're drenching my shirt! If you don't stop crying I'll be wet through!'

'I've sold the cottage,' she said, her face still buried in his shirt front. 'You were right, it is only bricks and mortar, and I don't know why I'm crying.'

'Feminine logic,' said Greg. 'Don't worry, I'm used to it. My mother uses that kind of logic all the time!'

She raised her head and looked at him accusingly. 'You're laughing at me,' she said.

His mouth curved into a smile. 'No, I'm not,' he said softly, 'and I know you've sold the cottage, because I've bought it.'

Pushing herself away from him, Abigail glared at him from arm's length. 'You!' her voice was accusing, 'you've bought it? How did you know it was for sale?' She began to feel angry, betrayed.

'Sister Collins told me you'd put in on the market, I found out which Estate Agents, and went there today in the theatre lunch break.' He fished some documents out of his pocket and waved them under her nose. 'I've got all the necessary pieces of paper. Of course,' he added, 'I am making one stipulation.'

'Oh, and what's that?' asked Abigail, feeling her anger begin to come to the boil.

'That the cottage is handed over to me complete. Lock, stock and barrel, all the furniture, plus a warm, loving wife.'

'A wife?' echoed Abigail weakly, wondering if her hearing was failing her.

'Yes, a wife,' answered Greg firmly, leaning forward and moving his lips slowly across her cheekbone. 'An impetuous, hot-headed, stubborn, sometimes bad-tempered, often infuriating English girl. Someone with whom life could never be dull.' He moved closer, pulling her towards him, pinning her arms to her side, as his lips sought the fluttering hollow in her throat.

Abigail felt as if her bones were melting. She had to know the name of the girl he had in mind. 'Her name?' she whispered, trying to keep a clear head, without success.

'Abigail,' he murmured, his mouth moving slowly, inexorably, towards her mouth, 'Abigail Pointer. I thought you would have guessed by now! Is there anything else you want to know?'

'Yes,' said Abigail, still struggling vainly to retain mastery of her senses. 'Why have you bought the cottage when you'll be returning to the States next year?'

'We shall be staying in England, darling, why else do you think I bought it? I've been offered a permanent post at the County General, and I've accepted. Any objections?'

'Yes, but . . .' Abigail began.

'Later,' said Greg firmly, lifting her up into his arms and carrying her into the lounge and plonking her on the settee. 'Now let me show you how much I love you.'

'Love? But I never thought . . .'

'Yes, love, love, love,' he said, kissing her between each word. 'You've driven me mad ever since we landed in a heap together in that milk, remember?'

'As if I could ever forget! But . . .' Abigail began to

kiss him back, with an enthusiasm matching his own, 'You never said anything about love, never gave me a clue. Are you sure you're not muddling it up with physical attraction?'

'At first, yes,' admitted Greg, cupping her face in his hands, 'but as time went on I began to realise that you'd got under my skin in a way no other woman ever has. There was only one problem, you were in love with Rupert, and engaged to marry him.'

'I *thought* I was in love,' corrected Abigail. 'I know now I was wrong.'

'Do you think you could love me?' asked Greg seriously his voice very soft. He hesitated, something unusual for him. 'Perhaps I've rushed you, perhaps . . .'

'Perhaps I already love you,' said Abigail, 'perhaps I've been too stubborn even to admit it to myself, but . . .' tenderly she traced the outline of his mouth.

'Only perhaps?'

'Well, I don't think I should succumb too easily!'

That was her last coherent thought, until much, much later.

ROMANCE

Next month's romances from Mills & Boon

Each month, you can choose from a world of variety in romance with Mills & Boon. These are the new titles to look out for next month.

THE RIGHT MAN Sandra Field
NO WAY TO SAY GOODBYE Kay Gregory
HIGHLAND TURMOIL Stephanie Howard
WITHOUT TRUST Penny Jordan
A PRICELESS LOVE Emma Darcy
JUST A NORMAL MARRIAGE Leigh Michaels
MAN WITHOUT A PAST Valerie Parv
WHEN THE LOVING STOPPED Jessica Steele
WHEN THE GODS CHOOSE Patricia Wilson
NO GENTLE LOVING Sara Wood
LOVE BY DEGREE Debbie Macomber
BUT NEVER LOVE Lynsey Stevens
A TAMING HAND Jenny Arden
HEIRS TO LOVING Rachel Ford

Buy them from your usual paperback stockist, or write to: Mills & Boon Reader Service, P.O. Box 236, Thornton Rd, Croydon, Surrey CR9 3RU, England. Readers in Southern Africa — write to: Independent Book Services Pty, Postbag X3010, Randburg, 2125, S. Africa.

Mills & Boon
the rose of romance

The latest blockbuster from Penny Jordan

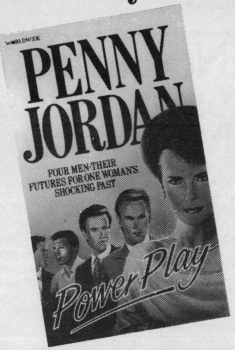

For Pepper Minesse, success as a young and powerful business woman has always been fuelled by one consuming desire – revenge against the 4 men involved in sadistically raping her in her teens.

Now she is ready.

She holds files that could destroy the lives and careers of these prominent men.

Together they must silence her – for ever.

Only one man's love can diffuse the insanity of the situation.

This blockbuster is Penny Jordan's most gripping and dramatic novel to date.
Nothing can beat POWER PLAY

Available: September   Price: £3.50

W☉RLDWIDE